UNREMEMBERING ME

BRAZILIAN LITERATURE IN TRANSLATION SERIES

SERIES EDITORS:
Dário Borim & Cristina Mehrtens

EDITORIAL BOARD:
Bela Feldman-Bianco
Lilianfontes Moreira
Robert Moser
Vivaldo Andrade dos Santos

UNREMEMBERING ME

Luiz Ruffato

Translated by
MARGUERITE ITAMAR HARRISON

TAGUS PRESS
UMass Dartmouth
Dartmouth, Massachusetts

Tagus Press is the publishing arm of the
Center for Portuguese Studies and Culture at
the University of Massachusetts Dartmouth.
Center Director: Victor K. Mendes

Brazilian Literature in Translation Series 6
Tagus Press at UMass Dartmouth
www.portstudies.umassd.edu
original Portuguese text © 2007 Luiz Ruffato;
translation and translator's note © 2018 Marguerite Itamar Harrison

Series Editors: Dário Borim & Cristina Mehrtens
Executive Editor: Mario Pereira
Copyedited by Amber Rose McCartney
Designed and typeset by A&A Publishing Services of NY, Inc. for
Integrated Books International

For all inquiries, please contact:
Tagus Press • Center for Portuguese Studies and Culture
UMass Dartmouth • 285 Old Westport Road
North Dartmouth MA 02747–2300
Tel. 508–999–8255 • Fax 508–999–9272
www.portstudies.umassd.edu

ISBN: 978-1-933227-84-9
Library of Congress Control Number: 2018954269
Library of Congress Cataloging-in-Publication Data
is available upon request

To Roniwalter Jatobá and Marçal Aquino

Contents

UNREMEMBERING ME

A Necessary Explanation

My mother came toward me as she dried her hands on her apron, took me in her arms, and in an unusual gesture, kissed my face, her eyes brimming with deep longing. My sister scooped up my daughter Helena, showering her with hugs and cuddles. My, how this girl has grown! Look how pretty she is! My father, still wearing his fraying hat, was absorbed in conversation with the cab driver. So, Mr. Moreira, how's business going? Lugging our suitcase to the concrete patio, my brother-in-law busily announced, I bought those two cases of beer and I found the best *cachaça*, you won't believe! February had been rough on the garden patch of roses, impatiens, geraniums, carnations, sunflowers, azaleas and hibiscus. Shirtless, sweaty boys abandoned their soccer game and leaned with curiosity over the walls surrounding our house. The rest of the afternoon was a flurry of visits from neighbors who darted in and out like hummingbirds.

We whiled away that Carnival around a rusty backyard barbecue that my mother's godson, Luzimar, manned from morning to night, grilling chicken wings, rib eyes and *linguiça* sausages. The greasy smoke seeped into the French roof tiles and clung to the perpetually-under-construction makeshift houses that extended along the ficus-streets of Taquara Preta. At all hours, there were raps at the gate and shouts of Anyone home?, my mother coordinating the comings and goings of relatives, acquaintances, friends. Is Luizim around? My goodness, how he's changed! And São Paulo, how about that? Is this your daughter? She doesn't look like you . . . And how about her mother? Oh, she couldn't come?! My niece tidied up the plates and silverware, upset with her husband who had withdrawn to the living room and stretched out on the couch, glued to the TV, as always.

Despite everything, we were a happy lot. Having gone to work at the Manufatora dye works early on, my brother-in-law felt the lack of opportunities and was prone to becoming moody for no reason. I knew that my sister's salary at the local school snack bar, along with her husband's meager earnings, made it hard for them to make ends meet each month. Ailing and frail, my father would trudge through every last corner of town selling crusty rolls, caramels, and doughnuts—twenty-five years earlier, Dr. Pace had gathered the entire family in Juiz de Fora: *I'm sorry to say, he only has about six months to live, unfortunately.* In the past, my mother took in as many as fifteen loads of laundry per week; her hands were still as bleach-burned as ever, but now they only had the strength to handle four. One Christmas I gave her a small wash basin, a novelty she showed off to the neighbors with great pride.

They lived on. She always kept a "travel bag" at hand—packed with a nightgown, a change of clothes, slippers, sandals, a hairbrush, a toothbrush and the necessary documents—"just in case" of whatever need that might arise with a ring of the telephone: some Ruffato from Rodeiro or Ubá who might be hospitalized or badly ill, or might have died; or who might be getting

married, or was about to be born, or baptized, or about to have
first communion or confirmation; or had had a disagreement
with their wife or husband or children, or whomever. Bemoan-
ing that My God, I'm so far away over here, she would lock the
door and stick the key in the hiding place and wait anxiously at
the bus stop for the bus that would take her to meet her kin. My
father was resigned, but he would still complain. So much as a
sneeze, and they call for her. He would wear out his ankle boots
(he only wore ankle boots), attending to those in the parish as a
way of musing about local politics—he was unfailingly anti-
establishment—reminiscing about old times, catching up on
news, and talking about nothing. Whenever he started a sen-
tence with, "Do you remember . . .," my mother would beat the
piece of clothing harder against the washboard and declare with
exasperation, "Here comes another rambling tale."

On Tuesday night, Luzimar parked his 1985 metallic-green
Chevette (nicknamed "Ole Clunker") on the sidewalk, accepted
the cup of coffee with cornbread my mother offered him, and
said he would take Helena and me to the bus station. My father
offered to go with us, but his godson discouraged him: he wanted
to show me the addition he was building first. It's going to be
Bruna's room, she's fifteen now and doesn't want to share with
Marcela anymore. And Soninha is coming with us, so there's not
enough room to fit everyone plus the suitcase. "Ole Clunker"
can't hold us all, she's getting old, poor thing. We said our good-
byes hastily, trying to avoid tears and sniffles. God willing, we'll
see each other again in no time.

At Luzimar's house in Ibraim, Helena stuffed herself with
Doritos and Coke, despite my warnings about the stench of the
toilet on the bus. You're going to have to pee and then we'll see
what happens . . . Luzimar and I checked out the construction
site, a two-by-three-meter rectangle, still just a pile of rebar, sand
and gravel, but soon . . . Next week we'll lay the concrete and put

in the bed, bedside table, wardrobe. Then, with the light off on the porch to keep the annoying termites away—fireflies flickering in the night, crickets gnawing away at the silence—he murmured, Soninha wants to speak to you. She suddenly appeared in the darkness, leaning back in a chair to take in the fresh air. Luiz, you don't think Godmother looks a bit thinner, do you? she whispered. She referred to my mother as "Godmother" as a form of endearment. I found the question odd, thought for a moment, but no, I wouldn't have any way to tell. Why? I don't know . . . She lost six kilos in a short amount of time . . . Six kilos?! Yeah, that's not normal, she pronounced, as a nurse's assistant at Cataguases Hospital. I was concerned and made them both promise to take my mother to a doctor. You know how she is, she never wants to be a bother. And I returned to São Paulo uneasy, the night sky throbbing with stars.

Even with all of us insisting—me, my sister, Luzimar, Soninha and my father—my mother only gave in and agreed to see a doctor at the end of March. She went to Dr. Wesley, who was young but had already built up a good reputation. He listened to her complaints, There's nothing wrong with me, I came because my family insisted, he listened to her with the stethoscope, inquired about her medical history, ordered an x-ray of her lungs, blood and urine tests, and a sputum culture, thinking of the tuberculosis that one day wore my father's health down. (*On sleepy early mornings: we would momentarily quicken our steps, my mother's determined, mine hesitant. The Viação Vitória bus would leave us in Juiz de Fora and we'd rush to catch another one that would drop us off in Santos Dumont, where my father was being treated, at the Palmira Sanatorium. One Sunday a month we'd make the journey. My mother would shower my father with hopes; I was stuck outside and would catch sight of him from a distance as I played amid the trees, squatting down to entertain myself with fire ants, beetles and geckos.*)

My mother finally agreed to a bronchoscopy at the Juiz de Fora Hospital during Holy Week, due to Dr. Wesley's dissatisfaction with the test results and the fact that she was plagued by coughing bouts that would dislodge her dentures. I'm only doing it to appease you. On that leisurely May morning, my sister and I walked in the direction of Aurora but toward nothing, leaving footprints in the yellow dust of the dirt road, the waters of the Pomba River and the wind and the birds whispering their silent secrets, every now and then a motorcycle, every now and then a car, veering away from pits and potholes, every now and then a bicycle. Good morning, Good morning, a landscape of dry leaves and fields, our solitude. The previous afternoon Dr. Wesley had explained the gravity of the situation: the cancer was spreading along its cruel, irreversible, stubborn and relentless course. Radiation therapy is painful and strenuous and would only create false hopes, I'm very sorry. It's better if she doesn't know, I said to my sister. We don't want her to suffer, right? I added anxiously, standing in the shade of a bamboo grove and handing her the morphine.

Helena spent part of her vacation at her grandmother's. Even debilitated, my mother tried to please her in every way, but any effort would leave her exhausted, her shaky hands gripping walls and furniture for support. Lying in bed, her anxious brown eyes feebly scrutinized the movement of the second hand on the alarm clock. What's happening to me, my son? she asked me when I came to pick up Helena at the end of July. Nothing, Mom, nothing serious, soon you'll be back on your feet and we'll go to Rodeiro, just the two of us, like we used to back when . . . I choked up and turned away, shouting impatiently, Helena, let's go, we're late!

Fifteen days later I was back in Cataguases: I went to see her in the hospital. Ignoring visiting hours, Soninha guided me through the dim hallways that exuded despair and suffering. She pointed me to her room, No, she's not at all well, it won't be long now. I pushed the door open slowly and was surprised to see her sitting up against the window, peering out at the bustle of the street, just skin and bones in her hospital gown. I whispered, Mom?! When she turned, I was shocked by the fear I saw on her gaunt face: death was already at the door and she was desperately trying to hang on to the invisible cord that keeps us alive, but it was rotting and crumbling in her sweaty hands. Oh, my son, I'll never be able to make that *taioba* with polenta you like so much ... I'm leaving you, my dear boy, I'm leaving soon ... I don't want to ... I don't want to ... What will happen to your father, all alone, poor thing? And to your sister? My god, oh my god ...

Speechless, I abandoned her there, a spirit floating on the mattress, and swiftly made it to the avenue of *oitizeiro* trees with my cowardice lapping at my heels. Drenched in pure sunshine, August was obliviously full of life, spreading leaves and dust particles, lazily goading the afternoon between clouds and irritated car horns. Under the *sibipiruna* trees at Rui Barbosa Square I slipped into the depths of childhood memories, *my sister couldn't stand the countryside, she thought it was for hillbillies, but my brother and I melted with happiness, my mother would stop at Pivatto to buy a sheet of the* caçarola *cake we would devour during the miles that lay ahead. We would greet the Italian folks who would clear the tobacco fields, plough the rice paddies, strip the rows of corn, the Bicios, the Michelettos, the Spinellis, the Benvenuttis, the Chiesas, the Prettis, the Finettos, the Justis, the Zoccolis, and so many more! My mother, wisely fending off jealousies, would split us up among our relatives' houses—I preferred Uncle Pedro's, who would wake us up with the scent of the* piada *flatbreads he would cook, one by one, for us to eat for breakfast. Tirelessly, she would traverse these places with happiness, exhaustively gathering and sharing news of the latest events since her last visit. In the orchard, she was determined to find the ripest oranges—her favorites were the sweet* laranja-limas. *The scent of popcorn on card game nights, screeches in the early mornings when a pig was slaughtered, laughter flowing on afternoons forever to be forgotten.* My mother is dying and the man who is talking to Mr. Pantaleone at the newsstand is totally unaware of it. The pregnant woman picking out items for her baby in the store up ahead, the stray dog scratching his pale fur, or the forlorn *churro* vendor, the old woman watching me from her window, the retirees in the bank line, the two friends drinking beer at the corner bar, the couple arguing discreetly, the child throwing a tantrum, the brown-and-beige-clad trio from Cataguases High School in their aloof adolescence, the young man smoking anxiously while waiting for someone, another eating ice cream, the motorcyclist and his backseat passenger, the beggar, the bicycles, the sparrows, the clouds—nearby, in a gloomy cubicle that smells of medicine, my mother is lying in agony in the late afternoon light. *My mother would break the chicken's neck, drain it, scald it, pluck it and quarter it as my grandmother had taught her. She dreamed of seeing the sea. One time we went to Marataízes, she had a brand-new bathing suit she refused to put on, embarrassed. She took off her sandals, stepped into the sand, and waded into the salty water, and said, Alright, and at her insistence we returned to Cataguases the next morning. On Sundays, the house full of people, she would toil for endless hours in the kitchen—"it's my pleasure, everyone's enjoying themselves."*

In 2001, the 7th of September—Independence Day—fell on a Friday. I took the long weekend to go visit my son Filipe in Belo Horizonte, where he was studying. The student residence was empty—his three roommates had gone to relieve their homesickness—and we spent the day on idle outings: beer and liver and eggplant appetizers at the Central Market, a movie at Diamond Mall, something or other at Pizza Hut. Sleep eluded me, aggravated by the red blinking neon sign on the building across the street, *Hotel Madrid*. The cell phone rang at five in the morning. It happened, my sister's broken-up voice jolted us awake, Filipe and I, in the dim light of daybreak.

The morning was just beginning to stir when we headed to Ubá, via Ouro Preto and Ponte Nova, deep in thought. The iron ore mountains, the cattle scattered over scorched fields, the receding rivers, the yawning towns, the passengers, my eyes seeing none of it—I was saying goodbye to other sojourns that had taken hold of my body at one time and were now being submerged forever more. Filipe's mother was waiting to take us to Rodeiro, where, after the open-casket mass at São Sebastião Church, we joined the funeral procession carrying the coffin to the family plot, my father braced against my sister for support. Before the cemetery attendant lined up the bricks to border the plot, I headed down the hill, distancing myself from the sad, gruesome cemetery, my friend Fernando Cesário leading me away to the shelter of his ranch on the Cataguases-Miraí Road.

My bare feet splash in a type of cave—the water or mud reaches my ankles—so dark that even with my eyes wide open I can't see my filthy hands groping the shadows. Cobwebs smash into my face, rats squeal in burrows, ravenous, flying cockroaches collide with my naked body. Something propels me forward, and as I advance I imagine steep banks collapsing behind me. I crawl ahead as the opening narrows and air becomes scarcer—whimpering voices guide my hopes. My thighs weaken, my temples twitch, my lungs burn. Strangely, I don't scream; the anguish seems to strangle me. Suddenly, I wrap my arms around my legs: I am ready.

On Sunday, hiding out on the porch, I caught the day by surprise. The rustling parakeets spilled glistening drops of dew upon the morning glories encircled by buzzing hummingbirds. Sparrows hopped in the moist grass. Double-collared seedeaters perched like puffs of cotton in the shade of the ironwood tree. A male saffron finch sought courtship in the corner of the garden.

Saddam, the foul-tempered mastiff, paced angrily in his cage—each of us expressing our mutual dislike for the other. I decided to move on, heading in the direction of the caretaker Gésus' house.

The dogs greeted me excitedly, alerting the girl who timidly rushed inside, abandoning the push broom she'd been using to clean the terrace. Pacifier in his mouth, the boy stared at me from behind the door to the living room. Gésus appeared with a cigarette dangling from his mouth, reprimanding his mutts. Shush, dumb dogs! He shook my hand, embarrassed. My condolences, Mr. Luiz, Doctor Fernando told us the news. Would you like a cup of coffee? The missus just made it fresh. We went in through the kitchen. Zezé, this is Luiz. Oh, how sad, Mr. Luiz, she said emotionally. Please come sit, sit here, she gestured to a chair. Her fingers wiped the plastic cover over the table, shooed away the flies, placed the thermos down, and took the tea towel off the covered plate to reveal a loaf of cornbread. I chewed a piece, the anise filling my mouth and bringing back the urge to smoke. *It only takes one drag, just one to . . .*

We left bundled up against the cold, the fog wafting over the valley beyond the barbed wire fence. Normally uncommunicative, Gésus made an effort to speak, perhaps feeling sorry for me. He held out his arms in the direction of the fish-breeding farm and said, Everything's empty over there! The *muçum* snake . . . a plague! We had to drain the tanks. At first, it was wonderful. We'd fish tilapia with our bare hands. Now . . . *Muçum*? Yeah, it's like a black snake that ravages the fingerlings . . . It's a plague! The winter dust was suffocating the feeble brush. At the ranch, he introduced me to the wet-nosed, brownish Gir calves; opening the gatepost, he goaded them up the hill. I followed him to a lean-to covered in French tiles, where he approached a rectangular concrete box and with his calloused hands brushed away the velvety layer of rotting straw on the surface to reveal giant writhing worms beneath. They're African, and they produce really good quality fertilizer. The tour took us to the orchid greenhouse, You should see how Doctor Fernando takes such care of them! To the orchard—they're seedlings, all the way from overseas. To the terrace, Sirley, please bring us some water, dear child.

Fernando parked the Ford Pampa. So, did you rest a bit? While we lit the grill, he apologized for not coming sooner. I thought you might want to be alone, he said, anticipating what I might say. He opened a bottle of beer to share, and we sat in silence around the now blazing fire. There was just an invisible song from a thrush, bits of conversation coming from Gésus' house, the rustling of bamboo. We spent what was left of that Sunday unhurriedly—death lurking in some nearby corner. The firewood turned to embers, then to charcoal, then to ash. The night blurred the edges of the world.

When night came I bunked at my sister's house; she placed a mattress on the concrete floor of the dining room and I dropped off immediately into much-needed sleep. The next morning we woke—she, my father, and I—to tend to an unspoken yet understood concern of my mother's, to take her meager belongings and donate them to the needy. I was in charge of combing through the empty house to separate and sort through items that were still hers but no longer hers to keep. My left hand plucked the key from the small recess below the eaves, and my right unlocked the modesty of that living room, so often visited but now so painfully unfamiliar. Standing on the marble center table, a bud vase displayed a plastic rose; on top of the cupboard, three picture frames showed off the grandchildren; the sofa and armchairs rested unused, the television set remained undisturbed— everything was blanketed with a thin layer of dust. The chairs in the kitchen sat motionless, a plaid cloth shrouded the table, anxious pans and plates confined to the steel cabinet, a beam of light searched in vain for the hustle and bustle—the room held its breath, as if actors waited in the wings.

In the bedroom I opened the wardrobe wide: draped on wire hangers, lonely dresses clung to one another fearfully, realizing that the woman they'd once served wasn't ever coming back. I put myself to the task before I could retreat in fright. I didn't fold skirts and blouses, nightgowns and trousers: I shoved them mechanically into two leather bags—in a paper bag I did the same with sandals, shoes and slippers. I was suprised by how little she had—I, who thought I knew her so well. I sifted through drawers of head scarves and intimate items, sheets and covers, towels and documents, photographs and mementoes.

Under the double bed, a forgotten small rectangular wooden box. I pulled it toward me and placed it on the chenille bedspread; opening it, interrupting Monday's wearying chores, I found where my mother had hidden her tattered heart. *My brother had announced, There's a company in São Paulo, they're hiring everybody, I think I'll go work there. Dumbstruck, my mother started shaking. My father said, If you think it's for the best . . . My sister and I just listened. He returned for good, seven years later, in a coffin that couldn't even be opened, his body was so mangled. An accident between Vassouras and Paraíba do Sul: all that was left of his new car were twisted pieces of metal. It's not right, my father whispered, for a father to bury his son, it's not right. Silent, my mother stopped raising chickens, stopped the Sunday dinners, stopped feeling joy. She became melancholic, withdrawn, shunning all futures-to-come.*

: the painted portrait of my brother; *For years it had remained there, watching us. A short, fat talkative man clapped his hands announcing, Hey there, is anyone home? I called to my mother, who offered him a glass of water and a cup of coffee on a stainless-steel tray covered in a white plastic lace doily, followed by countless refills.*

Months later, he solemnly presented the oval frame, a face that in no way resembled my bother's, a fact that irked my father but did not diminish my mother's delight, as she paid the agreed price and hung it with tenderness on the living room wall.

: the bench vise built by my brother, which she kept meticulously polished, proof that he'd finished the Senai course as a lathe operator in Cataguases;

: a bundle of letters, carefully tied together with string.

The portrait was lost; the vise rusted and became a toy for my great-nephew Hugo, and then disappeared; I took the letters with me, along with my mother's eyeglasses and an image of her beloved Saint Rita of Cascia, all to remember her, always.

The bundle of letters migrated from one piece of furniture to another untouched, succumbing unfailingly to the urgency of everyday futilities. Did I fear that by venturing into that wasteland of days gone by, I'd be swallowed up in a treacherous quicksand pit of memories? Perhaps. But most likely, I think I was stricken with pride brought on by jealousy. My mother made sure that the memory of her eldest son would not fade, and in this effort of resignation and self-deprivation, she drifted away from my sister and from me. I fought against this fixation that haunted me for nights on end, but its sting never left my skin.

At the end of 2003 I was packing up for yet another change of address—the twenty-sixth in my life—when I found the bundle of letters while taking books down from a shelf. I immediately sat on the dusty floor of the empty apartment and untied the string. There were fifty letters written by my brother to my mother, carefully arranged by date. Distraught, I went through each letter one by one, the pages filled with small cursive handwriting, recounting trivialities, asking for news. I summon this past*—as a means of bringing the dead to life, those who have begun to weigh on my heart: my brother, my mother, my father, whom I will meet again someday. This book is dedicated to them.

*I reproduce the letters here in their entirety, only taking care to update and correct the spelling and very rarely the punctuation. I have tried to maintain their quasi-colloquial style.

THE LETTERS

To you, who has already forgotten me

São Paulo, February 2, 1971

Dear Mom, dear Dad,

I've only just managed to sit down and write to you today, Tuesday. The trip went well, but I was really tired when I arrived. I had never traveled so long on a bus before . . . the worst part is that I couldn't sleep at all . . . and I even got kind of queasy. There was a woman who had her window open the entire time, complaining about the young guy next to her who wouldn't stop smoking. So the wind was hitting me straight in the face and kept me up the whole time. The person sitting next to me was a man named Gesualdo, who turned out to be the brother of Mr. Marciano, Mrs. Marta's friend, do you remember him, Mom? He said he knows you and Dad well. What a coincidence, huh? He got on the bus with me in Leopoldina and had come from Cataguases, but I hadn't noticed him before. He chatted with me a bit, but he fell asleep before we arrived in Porto Novo. The bus made three stops for people to use the restroom and get something to eat. I didn't get off at the first stop but I did get off at the second, mid-trip. It was an amazingly beautiful night and it gave me a lump in my throat, the thought that I might never see you and Dad again, or Luizinho and Lúcia, or my friends, or our home. But I know we have to work hard to improve our lives, and God willing, someday I'll come back and we'll do all kinds of things together.

Nilson was waiting for me at the bus station right on time. Who'd have thought, Mom, that mischievous kid who was always getting dirty in the Beco washing yard, and throwing rocks onto people's roofs, who everyone said would never amount to anything in life, that same Nilson is now a hard-working, responsible young man, and he's been helping me a lot in this initial period. The bus station is really beautiful. It's so big, you'd have to see it to believe it. It has a colorful roof and an escalator.

I was scared to death to go down it, but I felt embarrassed in front of Nilson, so I did it. It's actually not that bad, one of these days I'll go back and practice. Mrs. Glenda—or maybe it's Mrs. Brenda, I didn't quite catch her name, I asked Nilson but he doesn't know either, and he's been living here for five months, but it's so hard to understand her when she speaks that I don't know if it's Mrs. Glenda or Mrs. Brenda—she put me in the same room as Nilson. There are two bunk beds in the room. Tell Luizinho that he would love living here, he's crazy about bunk beds . . . I sleep on the bottom. Another guy sleeps on the top, from the way he talks I think he must be from Bahia. Nilson sleeps on the top of the other bunk bed, and then there's a quiet guy named Valdisnei, I don't know where he's from. The fact is, everyone here in the boarding house comes from somewhere else.

Tomorrow Nilson is going to show me how to get to Diadema, to the company I'm applying to. Pray that everything goes well.

So, how are you, Mom? And what about Dad, has his cough improved? Tell him I haven't forgotten his advice: I only talk to people who Nilson says are his friends or acquaintances. And how's Luizinho? He'd go nuts if he could see the number of people in this city. We left the bus station, caught a local bus, rode around for ages, caught another one, and only then did we make it here to Ipiranga. And Nilson says that's nothing, that I haven't seen a tenth of the city yet. It's unbelievable . . . How's Lúcia? Tell her I'll buy her her very own radio as soon as I can.

Mom, I'll stop here, otherwise this letter will go on forever. Please give my love to everyone, from your son who misses you very much,

José Célio

São Paulo, February 7, 1971

Dear Mom, dear Dad,

How's everyone over there? Today is Sunday and I'm taking advantage of the fact that everyone is still asleep to send you some news. People here wake up late on Sundays because they work so much during the week. I hardly see Nilson because he leaves really early, when it's practically still dark, and he doesn't get back until around seven at night.

Everything went well at the company, thank God. There was a huge line of people who wanted to work there, since it's a big factory. It's called Conforja, and there were people from all over Brazil. I stood in line for a long time, but as soon as the guy saw that I had been trained at Senai he gave me more consideration and told me I already had a spot. He said that qualified candidates are different and that being from Minas Gerais meant I was a good person. That made me really happy. He said this coming week I'll be called in and Nilson told me they'll definitely call me. The factory is far from the boarding house and if I do end up working there, then maybe later on, once I have a better sense of things, I'll move somewhere closer. The boarding house is really nice. Mrs. Glenda or Mrs. Brenda, I still don't know, is like a mother to everyone here. She takes care of each of us as if we were her own sons. And mind you, there are about ten of us living here. The linens are always perfectly clean and so is the floor. The problem is when you want to take a shower or use the bathroom. You can't take too long because there's always someone wanting to come in. She doesn't serve meals, just breakfast. I've been eating here in the neighborhood. Nilson showed me a place that serves set meals that aren't half bad. I've been careful with money because things are really expensive here. But I've been eating well, don't worry.

When you get a chance, please let me know how things are going with everyone over there. This afternoon Nilson promised we'd go for a walk around the area since the Ipiranga Museum is close by. That's where Emperor Pedro I declared Brazil's independence. Ask Luizinho if he's learned about that yet in school. Lúcia has, I'm sure.

I love and miss you all, from your beloved son,

José Célio

São Paulo, March 14, 1971

Dear Mom, dear Dad,

I received your letter, and I was so happy that I secretly cried. It's funny how we don't appreciate these kinds of things, but when we're far away we think differently or something, I don't know why. It was the first time I spent my birthday alone. I didn't tell anyone, but Nilson remembered. You must have mentioned it to him, Mom. He bought two family-size Cokes and Mrs. Glenda—I think it's Glenda after all—she made hot dogs and they even sang Happy Birthday. In the end, it was fun. At night I got sad and cried because I wished I could be there with all of you, but I know, like Dad says, we have to aim for a better life and we can't always choose the paths that will get us there. I told Mrs. Glenda that you were praying for her and she said thank you. She's a really good person. I've been working since February 15th and I've already gotten my first paycheck, that is, half of my first month's salary. Mom, you won't believe this but I'm making 748 *cruzeiros**! And the head of my division, a German man we call Mr. Volfe, told me if I work hard I'll be earning a lot more soon. In fact, that's why I didn't write sooner, because I'm working like crazy now. I start at 7am and leave at 5pm and I eat lunch right there at the company. The food's good, cafeteria-style, and there's something different every day. The older guys say I'll get sick of the food soon because it all tastes the same, but I disagree. Of course, it doesn't even come close to your food, Mom, which I miss so much, nothing in the world tastes as good, but the food here isn't bad at all. In my opinion, at least. But to get there at 7am I have to leave the house before 5am. I catch a bus to Vale do Anhangabaú and then another to Diadema. And I only get home around 7pm. It's really hectic, but I'm learning a lot. We

*Equivalent to four times the monthly minimum wage at the time.

leave Senai thinking we know everything, but in practice it's a different picture. The older guys have been really nice to me. Anything I don't know, they teach me. The supervisor, Mr. Válter, has been helping me a lot, he said pretty soon I'll have an official position.

I was so happy to hear that Luizinho knows the story of the cry for independence at Ipiranga. Of course, he's a pretty darn smart kid, isn't he? So, Lúcia has a boyfriend? I've got to see that ... No, I don't remember the guy, I know his brother, Remildo. But the family is well known. I hope Lúcia behaves herself. I'm saving up some money to go home and visit on Independence Day. The 7th of September will fall on a Tuesday, and the supervisor told me we can take vacation from Saturday to Tuesday, if we work some overtime hours and reach our quotas. We'll see. If I do go I'll bring each of you a little present. Think about what you might like to get, Mom.

With your blessing, your homesick son

José Célio

São Paulo, May 16, 1971

Dear Mom, dear Dad,

Forgive me for not writing sooner but the last two months have been really hectic. Time flies when you're far from home! When I was there I always thought time passed so slowly, and now the days just fly by . . . I received the two letters you sent me, Mom, but I really didn't have any chance at all to answer them. We're putting in overtime at work, and with the way things are going, God willing, I'll have some money saved up very soon. I'm still really homesick but I accept it more now. In the beginning—I can't lie to you, Mom—I got a little desperate. I missed everything from home and everything here was so foreign to me. Nilson and Mrs. Brenda—I think it's actually Brenda, not Glenda—they were even starting to worry about me. But, like you always said, Mom, work helps during these tough moments. I'm fine when I'm at work, but Sundays are the problem. Nilson takes me out with him when he can. Would you believe that I've even been to the zoo? In fact, tell Luizinho I saw some animals there he'd go nuts over. Lions, giraffes—you have no idea how big those things are, Mom—elephants, hippos, wow, so many animals. And the snakes? Those poor little snakes we'd kill out in the countryside aren't even as big as the baby snakes I've seen here. They're truly scary. It was a fun day. It was cool outside and we walked around all day long, there and back. We ate there at the zoo and drank *guaraná*. Nilson, who's a bit more adventurous, even started flirting with a girl, but in the end he didn't have the nerve to go over and talk to her. He joked that if I hadn't been there as the third wheel he would've talked to her, but I doubt it. He brags a lot but he's just as goofy as I am. Maybe a little less, I think, but only a little bit. Mrs. Brenda warned me to be prepared because it's getting colder, and when it gets cold here, it's no joke. You can already feel a chill in the early morning that makes your joints ache, but everyone says that's nothing, the real cold is coming soon. We'll see.

So, Lúcia's boyfriend comes over to the house now, is that right? Is Agnaldo a good match for her? I hope she takes this relationship seriously because when a girl dates around a lot, people end up talking, as you know. And she's old enough now to start taking life more seriously since she's turning 15 in June, isn't she? Tell Luizinho that Nilson and I are planning to go to Pacaembu Stadium to watch a soccer match one of these days.

Have you thought about your present, Mom? And how about Dad, what do you think he might want? Don't tell Lúcia, but I'm going to send her a little gold chain for her birthday. One of Nilson's colleagues is going to Cataguases in June and he already said he'll deliver some gifts for me. That's how it is around here, we all try to help each other out the best we can.

Alright, Mom, I'll stop here. I ask for your blessing and also Dad's. Goodbye for now.

Your beloved son,

José Célio

Diadema, August 8, 1971

Dear Mom, dear Dad,

It took me a while to write because I've moved in the meantime. It was getting really exhausting going back and forth from Ipiranga every day, so I ended up moving to a boarding house right here in Diadema. I was sorry to leave behind my roommates, especially Nilson, who has become a close friend of mine. In fact, tell Luizinho that the night before Lúcia's birthday the two of us went to watch the final of the Paulista Championship at Morumbi Stadium. São Paulo beat Palmeiras 1–0, with a goal by Toninho Guerreiro right at the beginning of the match. My goodness, I've never seen so many people all in one place in my life! It was terrifying. I was unnerved, I admit. But it was worth it, it was a great game. Just seeing all those players out there, who we'd only seen before in *Placar* magazine, live, up close, right in front of us . . . It was like a dream come true. So, Lúcia liked her little gold chain then! The girl at the shop who helped me pick it out thought she would like it. Women understand women, that's what I always say. But I'm sure going to miss Nilson's company, that's for sure. It's a shame, but I couldn't go on wearing myself out the way I was. Mrs. Glenda—I found out her name, one day I received a utility bill with her name on it, Glenda something, a really difficult last name. Poor thing, she was devastated because I think she lives alone, apparently she's a widow and doesn't have any children or relatives here, from what I gathered she's a foreigner and so she gets really attached to the people who live in her boarding house. She wished me all the best and she even cried when she saw me leaving with my suitcase, would you believe it? But I promised I'd go back to see her and Nilson and the other friends I made there. Now I'm living in a house that serves breakfast, lunch and dinner, but I don't eat lunch there, I eat at the factory. I'm always back there for dinner, though, because

Mrs. Sinoca is a great cook. Of course, she doesn't come anywhere close to you, Mom, but for a boarding house, the food is
actually pretty good.

I'm struggling to adjust to the cold here, like Mrs. Glenda
had warned me. Would you believe that sometimes when I wake
up in the morning the water won't even come out of the faucet
because it's frozen? It's true, Mom. The other day I saw some
boys scooping at the grass with a spoon and then eating it. I
thought it was funny so I went to ask them what it was, and they
laughed and told me it was snow. The grass had turned completely white with ice and they were eating that ice. It made me
want to eat some too, but I was embarrassed. I bought a sweater
in May, but it wasn't nearly enough. I bought another thicker one
and in mid-June I bought a cap and gloves and corduroy pants,
and a wool coat because I thought I was going to freeze to death.
When I would leave for work I couldn't see my own hand in
front of my face. Now it's getting better, but it's still really cold.
The guys at the factory laugh their heads off at me because I said
that in times like these I just want to run away, grab my things at
the boarding house, hop on a bus and go back to Cataguases. At
least it's not so cold there.

Mom, I'm sending you a little money with this letter, so you
can buy whatever you might need over there at the house. This
isn't the present I promised yet, I'll bring that to you in person
next month because, God willing, in less than a month I'll be
there, and it will be a day of pure joy! Go ahead and start prepar-
ing the *taioba* and the layered cookie pie because when I get
there I'll be dying to eat all those things only you know how to
make (can you believe that no one here has heard of *taioba*?).

Respectfully, with a kiss on the hand for you and for Dad,
your son

José Célio

Diadema, September 26, 1971

Mom, Dad,

I've finally been able to sit down today and write to you in peace. I was so happy, you can't imagine how happy I was to see you again, and Dad, and Lúcia and Luizinho, and our friends. Those days were just perfect. I never imagined someone could miss their loved ones so much. I must confess to you, Mom, it was really hard to get on that bus and come back to São Paulo. When I was in Leopoldina waiting for the bus to arrive from Alegre—jolly name for a city, isn't it?—I was feeling so terribly sad, I just sat in a corner like a fool, and had this urge to just grab my bag and go home and hug you and Dad, and Lúcia and Luizinho, and say, no, I don't want to go back there. But I knew I couldn't do that. We don't get to choose our destinies and it's my duty to try to earn a living here in São Paulo. But it's not easy.

I'm worried about Dad's health. Coughing like that and spitting up blood is not normal at all. He has to find another doctor because that Doctor Romualdo is bad news. He's more concerned about politics than anything else. I don't know why Dad trusts him so much. I already talked to him, but you're the one who can get through that thick skull of his. Please keep me posted, Mom, because I'm really worried. Lúcia hasn't changed: did you see how mad she got just because I mentioned the length of her miniskirt? It's inappropriate, plain and simple, and I won't just look the other way. I apologize for the trouble our argument caused, but don't you agree that it's unacceptable? For heaven's sake! Legs on display, nail polish, lipstick, God forgive me for saying this, but she looked like a hussy. That's why no one wants to go steady with her. Later on when she regrets it, it'll be too late. I enjoyed seeing Luizinho. He's studying a lot and when I asked him a few questions he had all the right answers. He seemed to like the button soccer game I gave him, don't you think?

Things are moving along here. The company promised me a raise for November or December. Mr. Volfe said the orders are better than they expected, so . . . Would you believe I got cold on the trip back? It's like an icebox here.

Mom, please keep me updated on how things are going with Dad because I'm worried about him.

I love you and miss you, from your beloved son,

José Célio

Diadema, October 3, 1971

Mom,

I'm worried sick about Dad's hospitalization. I knew it wasn't normal to be coughing up bloody phlegm, I just knew it. Who would've thought it would be tuberculosis? I really wish I could be there by your and Dad's side to try to help out in some way. But I went to talk to Mr. Volfe, who has been like a father to me, and he discouraged me from dropping everything here and going back to Cataguases. He said that now more than ever you all need me here so I can send you money for you to support Lúcia and Luizinho. He even told me he would move up my salary raise so that I would have it already on this month's paycheck, and I didn't know what to do. This kind of thing would take the wind out of anyone's sails. I'm so sad about all this, I can only imagine how you're feeling. You said he'd have to stay in Santos Dumont for six months, but does that mean he won't be able to visit any of you for six months too? Where exactly is Santos Dumont? Why does he have to be somewhere so far away, isn't there a sanatorium closer? Mom, I don't even know what to think right now. God give us the strength to get through this ordeal.

I'm sending some money with this letter so that you can take care of things for the time being. I'll send more as soon as I can, and God willing at the end of the year I'll come home and go with you to visit Dad.

I ask for your blessing, from your beloved son,

Célio

Diadema, November 2, 1971

Mom, dearest,

Today is All Souls' Day and I know how much this holiday means to you. I wish I could be with you right now, to go with you to the cemetery in Rodeiro to visit our family's dead, Grandpa and Uncle Olavo, to be with you during this time of sadness and remembrance. But, unfortunately, Mom, I'm so far away, so alone and feeling so useless, because I can't even go and be with Dad in Santos Dumont. You said that it's not possible to visit him every Sunday, only once a month, but I'm upset that Lúcia doesn't go with you. Luizinho is still so little, poor kid, and he's the one who has to go along. Is he behaving himself? And do you think Dad is getting any better? I talked to Mr. Volfe and he said nowadays tuberculosis isn't such a serious problem anymore, but he recommended—and actually the company doctors insisted—that I be tested for TB, and so I did, and it was negative, of course. But he asked me if you, Lúcia and Luizinho have been tested because it's important since tuberculosis is contagious, but Mr. Volfe said these days the treatment is really good and people usually make a full recovery. He said Dad will leave the sanatorium better than when he came in. I was wondering how Dad caught this illness, poor thing, he must be suffering a lot, being so far away from us, from you, and for someone like him who can't sit still, being stuck there, all alone, with nothing to do, it must be really hard on him.

I'm going to church today and I'm going to pray for Grandpa's soul and Uncle Olavo's, and for Dad's health, too.

Send my love to everyone, from your son

Célio

Diadema, January 9, 1972

My dear Mom,

I returned to Diadema with an aching heart. Those days spent with you and Luizinho and Lúcia, and our trip to Santos Dumont to see Dad, even though it was a short visit, it all left a deep mark on me. I didn't want to come back, I swear, and I only did so because you insisted, and rightly so. It's true now more than ever that you and the kids need my financial support. But at the same time, I was happy to see that Dad had gained weight and had a rosier complexion. It's a shame he still has to stay in the sanatorium until April. The doctor didn't give an exact date? But, like you said, sometimes bad things are a blessing in disguise, who knows if this isn't just something that will bring us all back together so we can be happy again, somewhere down the road? Luizinho has grown up and seems to have a good head on his shoulders, but Lúcia just won't stop her bickering, it's almost like she doesn't learn from her own suffering. Sometimes I think she's got a rough road ahead of her in life, poor girl.

I really miss being in the countryside. There are a lot of gypsies around here and everyone's afraid of them. I remember we used to be scared to death when they would camp in Beira-Rio and everyone said they would snatch up children and disappear. One time, I don't know if you know this, I was in the countryside and went with Uncle Olavo to Rodeiro and there was a camp there somewhere around Quiabo Street. Uncle Olavo teased me and said he was going to trade me in for some horses and I got so scared that he had to buy me a *guaraná* soda so I would stop crying. He spent the rest of the time trying to butter me up. It ended up working out well for me, actually.

Mom, I spoke with Mr. Volfe and the company is going to buy out my vacation time. This way I can send money for you to pay all those unsettled bills and buy school supplies for Lúcia and Luizinho. God willing, next year I'll be able to take a few days off.

Goodbye for now, with your blessing, your son

Célio

Diadema, April 2, 1972

Mom,

Thank you for the shirt and for the green papaya jam and the cheese. It all arrived just fine. I stopped by Mrs. Glenda's boarding house yesterday, and would you believe that since I left, and it's been a while now, that was the second time I've gone back? She called me heartless and said I must not have liked staying there. I actually felt sorry for her, poor woman, she gets so attached to us. She went to the trouble of making a fresh pot of coffee and going to the bakery to buy cookies, which they call biscuits here. She was so excited that you remembered her and she asked me to thank you for the *doce de leite*. She said the *doce de leite* from Minas has no equal anywhere else on earth. And remember she's a foreigner. I was really happy to hear that Dad will be going back home soon. I'd love to go there and surprise him when he gets home, but I don't think I'll be able to. Work has been tough at the company and Mr. Volfe has really been pushing us. Nilson is all happy because apparently he's dating someone over there. I don't know if you know her, her name is Toninha, Mrs. Olga's daughter from the Beco, do you remember? He says his goal is to save some money to buy a plot there in Paraíso and then build a house in a year or two. As for me, I'm not even thinking about things like that. I still have a long way to go. Until Dad is fully recovered from this whole ordeal, I don't even feel like dating. I'm fine being on my own for now. Later on I plan to get married, have kids, give you a bunch of grandchildren. Mrs. Glenda wanted me to spend the night at the boarding house, but I left on the last bus and got home late. I got up really early today, ate some of the papaya jam with cheese, which was so delicious, and it suddenly gave me the urge to go walk around outside. The entire neighborhood is under construction, it's unbelievable. The streets are made of dirt, this red dust that sticks to your clothes, and the bus that goes downtown is even called "Dusty." I counted three volunteer housing projects right here next to one another. I walked and walked and then ended up stopping to watch a game of pick-up soccer, and this huge wave of sadness hit me because I feel like I don't belong here, and it was a beautiful day, mind you, full of sunshine and people selling popsicles and children running around ... And it made me think: no matter how much you try to adapt, there's really only one place you can call home, and that's just the way it is.

Well, Mom, no need to worry, I'm fine now. The day is ending and I'm ending this short letter too since it's already getting too long.

I'll be waiting to hear news about Dad.

I'm sending you some money with this letter so that you can do something nice for Dad when he gets home.

I miss you.

Your son

Célio

Diadema, April 9, 1972

Mom,

What a surprise! I came home from work yesterday and saw your letter and I opened it as soon as I stepped into my room. So you're saying Dad's already home! That's great! Take the money I sent you last time and throw him a little party. I was happy to hear that he's gained back some weight and gotten some color back in his face. That's a sign of good health, like Mrs. Sinoca says. She makes us eat a hardboiled egg every morning because she says it's a surefire remedy. How can he take all those 25 pills at once? When will he be able to go back to work?

Things are going well here, thank God, so don't worry. The papaya jam you sent was gone in a flash. Arnulfo, a roommate of mine, asked to try it and then went around telling everyone it was the best papaya jam he'd ever had in his life, and so then, of course, everyone wanted some. But it was good because we had a great time, just acting like a bunch of kids. Mrs. Sinoca asked if you wouldn't mind sending the recipe so she can try to make it the same way. It won't be the same because that's impossible, but she could come close. So, if you could send the recipe, that would make her really happy.

Mom, I'll say goodbye for now. Big hugs for everyone and please give my love to Dad, from your beloved son,

Célio

Diadema, May 28, 1972

Mom,

I don't know what happened, but I sent you a letter at the beginning of the month and it must have gotten lost. Mrs. Sinoca told me this happens a lot and she said she was even surprised that your letters always arrive without a hitch. All is well here, thank God. This morning I went out with Arnulfo and we went for a walk to see the construction work on the metro. They say it's going to be amazing when it's finished. To be honest, it's hard to imagine what it will be like. It's an underground train, so it's a bit weird to think about going underneath the street ... He said he's got a friend working there who goes for days without seeing the sun, can you believe it? Arnulfo is a good guy. He's from the Northeast, Pernambuco, I think, and he got here right around the same time I did, maybe a little earlier. We're like best friends now. Tell Luizinho we're planning on seeing the Brazilian national team play in the Independence Cup in July. Can you imagine? Everyone at work is talking about it.

I ask for your blessing, your son

Célio

Diadema, July 1, 1972

Mom,

I'm writing this letter with gloves on because the cold is unbearable. I'm sorry for the delay in responding, but I come home so tired from work I don't have the energy for anything else. Mr. Válter, our supervisor—I think I told you about him before—has helped me a lot at Conforja. He's been inviting me for some time now to come over to his house, in a neighborhood called Casa Grande. Sunday before last I went there. Mrs. Germana, his wife, prepares lunch for a bunch of people. She says since we're all from somewhere else, we're all family here. It's her way of doing things, to gather people at her house so we'll feel less lonely. They've been doing this for years, but from now on Mr. Válter tells me I'm also part of the family now. They have a huge house, still unfinished. They still need to plaster the walls and the concrete floor is still rough. Mr. Válter was showing me around and pointing out how he reinforced the structures so later on he can add a second floor. That way his children can live nearby. Mr. Válter is a good man and even though he's the company supervisor, everyone there respects and likes him. Mrs. Germana is also a nice person, she's a bit plump, with a dusky complexion, you know. They're from Ceará, I think, I'm not really sure. I tell you all this, Mom, so you'll see I'm gradually fitting in. They have three children, more or less the same age as at our house. Nena—that must be her nickname—is about 17. Eliane must be about 11 or 12 and Fabinho around 20 or 21. He's already working at Conforja, but in a different department from mine.

Tell Luizinho that tomorrow a group of us from work are going to the Brazil match against Yugoslavia, at Morumbi Stadium. Tell him to listen to the game on the radio because we're going to cheer like crazy every time Brazil scores a goal.

Give my love to Dad. I miss you very much, Mom.

Célio

Diadema, July 16, 1972

Mom,

It is so cold here! In the morning when I go to work you can't even make out your own hand in front of your face. It's unbelievable. And when I come back late in the afternoon, it starts getting foggy and this chill creeps in that's just dreadful. Some days I can't even take a proper shower. I'm embarrassed to admit that, but it's the honest truth.

Last Sunday we had the biggest celebration here at the boarding house. As soon as the soccer match between Brazil and Portugal at Maracanã Stadium was over, we went out into the streets to celebrate.* There were firecrackers, everyone hugging each other, just pure elation. Mrs. Sinoca drank some *caipirinhas*. I had never seen her drink before. Then she grabbed a pan and went outside and started banging it with a ladle, it was really funny. We all stayed up late talking and had a hard time going to work the next day.

Tell Luizinho I went to watch Brazil and Yugoslavia at Morumbi Stadium. Did he listen to it on the radio? I went with a big group from work. We cheered the whole time and made lots of noise for Brazil's three goals. I went with Mr. Válter in his car, but it got a flat tire so we had to get out and start walking until we found a tire shop because he didn't have a spare and the weight of the car could damage the tire rim. It took a really long time and when we got back here to Diadema it was already late at night. But it was fun. Someday I want to bring Luizinho here to visit and take him to the stadium so he can see how big it is, so big that every single person in Cataguases would fit inside with room to spare. I'm not lying, Mom, I wish you could see it.

*On July 9, 1972, Brazil won the Independence Cup with a 1–0 victory over the Portuguese national team in the championship match.

So it's true that Lúcia broke up with Agnaldo? She's truly hopeless, that girl. I hope God guides her down the right path because otherwise I honestly don't know what will become of her.

Mom, I'm sending you a little money along with this letter. I'd like you to buy a starter ball for Luizinho. I know how important it is for a kid to have his own ball because it commands respect, and the only people who succeed in this world are the ones who command respect from others.

Give my love to Dad.

Sending you a big hug, I miss you, your son,

Célio

Diadema, October 15, 1972

Dear Mom,

It's been a while since I've written, please forgive me, but I've been so busy here, you wouldn't believe it. I was really sad to hear Lúcia has stopped going to school. She could at least finish 8th grade, because these days you can't amount to anything if you don't have an education. I'm actually thinking about starting a mechanical drawing correspondence course through the Brazilian Universal Institute. I've even talked it over with Mr. Válter and he said it's a good idea because it would allow me to grow in the company. And to think Lúcia is quitting school, I just can't understand it. By the time she realizes how big of a mistake she's making, it will be too late. You know that pretty soon she'll get married, from there it's nothing but kids and responsibilities, and she'll never have time for anything. I'm going to write to her, we'll see if it does any good. She's like Dad, as hardheaded as they come.

Mom, I have something funny to tell you. Remember Nena? I told you about her, she's Mr. Válter's daughter. Her real name is Esmeralda, but she hates that name. When someone asks her what her name is, she says it's Nena. Then if you ask if that's her nickname, she says no, she says it's her real name. But the other day Mrs. Germana told me she's actually called Esmeralda, which I think is a pretty name, but Nena gets upset if people call her Esmeralda. I think Esmeralda is a beautiful name, it's a precious green gemstone. Isn't it funny for a person not to like their own name, especially when it's such a pretty one?

God willing, I'll come home for Christmas and New Year's. I'm going to bring presents for everyone. I'm thinking about buying a wristwatch for Dad, what do you think? The other day

I saw a really nice one with a steel band. Do you think Dad would like it?

Goodbye for now, a big hug for you, I miss you, your son,

Célio

Diadema, October 29, 1972

Dear Mom,

As they say, a mother's instinct is always right. How did you know I was in love with Nena? No, we're not dating. I mean, we've gone out a few times. The other day we went to the fair at the Bom Jesus de Piraporinha Church, another time we spent a Sunday afternoon sitting on the grass by the Rodovia dos Imigrantes roadway. But we're not dating yet. Mr. Válter knows and so does Mrs. Germana and they're very supportive, but we're still in that phase of getting to know each other better. Esmeralda is a really nice girl, very respectable, nothing like those friends of Lúcia who are always all dolled up. She doesn't like beer and she's not into Carnival, just studying. Would you believe she's finishing up her second year of high school? Don't tell Lúcia that, it might make her jealous. Or better yet, go ahead and tell her, maybe she'll change her mind about this whole thing of quitting school. I wrote to her, did she tell you that?

I'll bring the watch to Dad at Christmas, then.

Goodbye for now, I miss you,

your son, Célio

Diadema, November 12, 1972

Mom,

Lúcia's got some nerve. Can you believe she wrote me a letter telling me to mind my own business, that she's her own person in charge of her own life? That really upset me because I was just trying to help, as you know. Some of us have more experience, we know things aren't easy. What's the point of her getting a job at the Manufatora to earn such measly wages? She says that with her salary she'll be able to look more put together and before you know it she'll find herself a rich husband and a house and no one will be able to bother her anymore. What a fantasy! She'll be punching a time card for the rest of her life, poor girl. But, if that's what she wants, that's her problem. I'm not going to say another word.

So, Dad is slowly getting back into the swing of things? Thank God he's strong. He doesn't look it, but he's got the heart of a lion. Always has, hasn't he? I didn't remember Mrs. Eusébia's business that makes pastry cones. If it will be good for him and there's no harm in it, I think it's okay for him to sell them, sure. It'll give him something to do and it might even help a little with the expenses at home.

So, Luizinho made it through the school year? This kid is really going places! My dream is to see him go to Senai. As smart as he is, he'll have no trouble passing the entrance exam. For now he needs to be encouraged. You should always talk to him about it so he'll work hard at his studies because that's the only way to get ahead in life. I was thinking, God willing, by the time he's done with school I'll have a better position here at Conforja and I'll find him a good job, and then the two of us could work together. I can't wait to have someone else from the family here with me. It just gets so lonely.

Esmeralda and I are still seeing each other. I think we're going to end up making it official soon.

Goodbye for now, Mom, I love and miss you all,

your son, Célio

Diadema, January 28, 1973

Mom,

As soon as I got back here I got caught up in the rush of things. That's why I've only had time to sit down and write to you now. It was so great to be able to spend Christmas and New Year's with all of you. I hadn't felt so happy in a long time. Dad is doing better than I expected. I was surprised to see how much he liked the watch. And it wasn't even that expensive. I talked to Luizinho a lot. One day we were sitting up on the rooftop talking and before we knew it, it was already nighttime. We hadn't even noticed. He's dying to start at Senai and was imagining what it would be like to live here in Diadema. I thought that was great. I'm not worried about him at all because I think he's heading down the right path, thank God. And Luzimar! He's gotten so big, Mom! It had been ages since I'd seen him. But, by the look of things, he doesn't like school, right? That's a problem. But he's still young and he still has time to change his mind. Lúcia's the one who's really changed. We hardly spoke to each other. What an opinionated girl, Mom. She only thinks about dating, clothes and listening to the radio. I actually regret giving her that little radio. She didn't even thank me for it.

Mom, I finally worked up the courage to ask Mr. Válter if I could date Nena, and he and Mrs. Germana were so happy that they're going to throw a party at the end of the month to officially announce that we're together, can you believe it? No one else knows about it for now. I'm really happy, truly. I think I've found the love of my life. I'm even thinking of buying a plot of land, slowly paying it off and maybe somewhere down the line starting to build a little house. We have to think about the future, right? I'm dying to introduce her to you and Dad, but that will have to wait a bit. I'm sure you and Nena will get along really well. In any case, I'd like to have your approval, Mom.

Sending you a big hug, I ask your blessing, from your beloved son,

Célio

Diadema, February 25, 1973

Dear Mom,

The official announcement of my relationship with Nena was a huge celebration. And here's the best part: Mr. Válter agreed and Mrs. Germana is coming with me to take Nena to meet you for the holidays. She's bringing Eliane along too, you're going to love all of them. We'll only be staying for about 10 days because Mrs. Germana doesn't like to leave Mr. Válter and Fabinho on their own for too long. She says they're hopeless without her . . . Mr. Válter says he can cook, but she jokes that the only thing he knows how to do is fry an egg . . .

Mom, I'm worried about where we'll put everyone up. So, I'm sending a little money with this letter for you to buy two twin mattresses and some linens. Nena can sleep in Lúcia's room. Do you think she'd let Nena sleep in her bed and then she'll sleep on a mattress on the floor? See if you can convince her. We can put Mrs. Germana in Luizinho's room with Eliane. And Luizinho can sleep on the couch in the living room. I'll sleep in the living room too, on that fold-out cot. What do you think? Do we have enough chickens there to feed everyone? Mom, if you need anything just ask Mr. Zé Pinto to lend you some money and I'll pay him back later.

I'm really happy that you and Dad will get to meet Nena. I hope you'll approve of our relationship. I'm just afraid of Lúcia's reaction. Do you think she'll behave herself? We can't look bad because Mr. Válter's family is very distinguished and I want to make a good impression. We'll all be one big family soon, after all.

Mom, I know you'll understand that I'll be traveling back to Diadema with them. We're leaving here on the 9th, a Friday, and we'll arrive in Leopoldina early on Saturday, the 10th. Then we'll head back on Sunday night, the 18th.

I hope everything goes well.

Goodbye for now, give my love to everyone, from your be-loved son,

Célio

Diadema, May 1, 1973*

Mom,

Would you believe Mrs. Germana is still talking about our trip to Cataguases? She really liked you a lot. And that's the way she is, always very straightforward: if she doesn't like someone, she'll say it to their face. Mr. Válter had a car accident the other day, it wasn't serious, but he missed a few days of work. He's better now. I'm going over to their house in a bit, and from there we're all going over to Vila Euclides to celebrate May Day. They have all kinds of festivities there, with concession stands and a soccer tournament. I'm going to play for Conforja's first team. The other day Mr. Volfe, who has two left feet, told me that if I had dedicated myself to soccer I could've been a real star. But his opinion doesn't really count because he doesn't know anything about sports.

Mom, I'm going to stop here so I won't be late. I've been trying to toe the line lately because I want to be more attractive to Nena. I'm even using cologne, who would've thought? Speaking of which, she wanted me to tell you she says hi. Ask Mr. Pinto if the money got to him alright.

Give my love to everyone, from your loving son,

Célio

*It's likely that a previous letter was misplaced or got lost in the mail as there are no further comments about Nena and her family's visit to our house in March of 1973. I remember those days very well; they were filled with hustle and bustle and surprises. Lúcia behaved perfectly, not only giving up her bed, but also becoming close to her sister-in-law. Mrs. Germana and my mother spent the days talking for hours on end, despite some pangs of jealousy arising later on. I fell in love with Eliane, passion giving way to distance: my first kiss, my first farewell.

Diadema, August 5, 1973

Mom,

I have to tell you I was pretty upset to hear about Dad leaving the church. I never imagined he would become an evangelical ... I don't have anything against evangelicals but, honestly, everyone in our family has always been very Catholic and I don't think our relatives will take kindly to this change of his. But maybe it'll be short-lived. Let's pray that God will guide him back. I understand when he says the Crusade pastor showed him other paths, that's fine, but I honestly don't see any good coming from this. But, as they say, to each his own. In terms of smoking, he quit because of the treatment he had over at Palmira. As for drinking, he would only drink a bit of *cachaça* now and then, which never hurt anybody, on the contrary, it's actually supposed to be good for your health, everyone knows that. So, what did the pastor say to him that was so different? Sometimes I wonder if it isn't just Dad's stubbornness, he never got along with your family, right? I can't recall a single time when we were in the countryside that he was there with us. That's right, he would stay in Cataguases to work, but he didn't come with us even once. And you of all people know how hardheaded Dad can be. My hope is that he'll realize how foolish this is and the priest will welcome him back. This is so sad, Mom, and sets such a bad example for Luizinho. I won't even mention Lúcia, because at least in this situation she knows what she wants. I don't see her giving up her lifestyle of listening to music on the radio, strolling around the town square on the weekend, wearing those ridiculous clothes she wears, all to grow her hair out and start wearing those long-sleeved dresses and full-length skirts. Can you imagine Lúcia dressed like that? It's kind of funny to think about. But Luizinho is impressionable, we have to keep an eye on him. Especially since you said he's been tagging along with Dad. That's really serious, Mom.

Everything's fine here, thank God. Everyone at Mr. Válter's house sends their regards. I ask for your blessing,

your son, Célio

Diadema, October 7, 1973

Mom,

Unfortunately, life isn't always a bed of roses. I had a serious argument with Nena and I think we might break up. She told me that as soon as she finishes high school, now at the end of this year, she's thinking of going on to college. I don't have anything against that, of course, but I honestly don't want her to get a job somewhere else. People might think I'm old-fashioned, which is what she says when she criticizes me for saying something she doesn't like, but you know me, Mom, I can't stand these modern ways. And here I was thinking it was great that she doesn't like beer or Carnival. I thought she could be the ideal woman to care for our children, but now I see that I'm mistaken. She said she wants to be a teacher, now just imagine, Mom, if a teacher will want to marry a factory worker like me. The first chance she gets she'll kick my butt to the curb, pardon my language. I don't know what to do, Mom. Sometimes I think I should just go live out in the middle of the woods with all the animals because that's where I belong. I try to adapt to everything: to my job, to the city, to the people, but honestly, deep down I'm still just a dirt-poor nobody, who's afraid of everything and everyone. I'm sorry to dump all this on you but I don't have anyone else to talk to. I don't have any real friends here, and the only thing I do is work, work, work.

We keep forging these paths of ours, thinking we're moving forward, then suddenly you look up and see that you're actually lost ... And as the saying goes, when it rains, it pours. I keep thinking about Lúcia, how she has her head in the clouds, and Dad who's converted now, and you having to deal with everything on your own ... It's not easy, Mom, it's not easy at all.

I ask for your blessing, your son*

*Curiously, this is the only unsigned letter.

Diadema, October 14, 1973

Mom,

I'm writing this short letter just to let you know that Nena and I have worked things out. Don't worry. I'm sorry for dumping all that on you, but things seem to be fine now. We had a good talk and Nena told me she'll look for a teaching job for next year right here in Diadema, and her goal is for us to save up some money to buy a small plot of land and build a house later on. She's a really good person and a good companion, pretty wonderful, in fact. Can you believe we even talked about getting engaged next year? And Mrs. Germana said at the end of this year Mr. Válter is taking a vacation and we're all going to meet his relatives in Ceará because he wants to introduce me to everyone there. The town is called Irauçuba, it's in the interior of the state, where it's really dry. Would you believe it takes more than two and a half days to get there from here? And we think Cataguases is far away.

Is Dad still caught up in that evangelical nonsense? Keep an eye on Luizinho, Mom!

Hugs and love to everyone.

Célio

Diadema, December 15, 1973

Mom,

As I mentioned, this year I won't be spending Christmas and New Year's with you all, unfortunately. I got some time off from work and I'm headed to Ceará tomorrow, Sunday. Everyone went ahead of me, at the beginning of the month, so I'm here by myself. I've been using these days off to rest a bit since I've been working so much. We're stepping up the pace to deliver the end-of-year orders and so I've even been putting in some overtime. I also took the time to stop by Mrs. Glenda's boarding house last week. She was so happy and even cried, poor thing. She asked about you and Dad, and she was really surprised to hear that I'm in a serious relationship. She said that I'm still so young and should take more time to enjoy life for a while before thinking about marriage. Mrs. Glenda has some wild ideas! Nilson isn't living there anymore. Mrs. Glenda said he lost his job and got another one in São Miguel Paulista, so it was just too far away. She said he drops by once in a while, more often than I do. She doesn't understand that I have all these commitments. I heard Nilson is still dating Toninha. Have you seen her around? Mrs. Glenda says he's thinking of bringing her here, but not now, later on. She says despite their relationship, Nilson still enjoys life. He goes to dance parties and has little flings. She doesn't realize that I'm against that kind of thing. If he's dating Toninha, and he's serious about her, he can't be doing all that. Or maybe he's just stringing her along.

Mom, I'm sending you some money with this letter. Spend it as you see fit. If things get tight, then use it to pay the bills, and if anything is left over, buy a little something for everyone. If you're doing okay, buy something nice for yourself and something for Dad and Luizinho. For Lúcia too, if you can.

I ask for your blessing and please pray that everything goes well on my trip.

From your beloved son,

Célio

Diadema, January 13, 1974

Mom,

How are you? How's Dad? And Lúcia? And Luizinho? I hope you're all doing well and enjoying good health and happiness. I miss you all very much. It's really hot here now and sometimes it's even hard to fall asleep at night. But it's not as bad as it can get over there. I remember the times when I'd grab the mattress to go sleep out on the porch because it was so hot. Or when we'd get the mattress wet and lie down on it. All we actually managed to do was to rot the straw filling. We do some pretty dumb things when we're young, don't we?

Mom, the trip was really good. I met Nena's relatives in Irauçuba, actually in a place called Capim Açu. You wouldn't believe how many people were there, and they even told me that there used to be a lot more, but they left because of the drought and are spread all over God's great world. I was shocked by the poverty there. Everywhere you look, it's completely dry. There's no proper water to drink, no food to eat, nothing. I don't know how anyone survives there. People say it's out of stubbornness. It's really heartbreaking: a few scrawny cows, some scrawny dogs, starving kids with distended bellies. I spent a lot of time talking to Fabinho. I hadn't talked to him that much before. We only saw each other at the Sunday lunches and our conversations were only about soccer, work, that sort of nonsense. But Fabinho is a seriously smart guy. He told me the higher-ups are to blame for all the poverty. He said that when the government sends supplies for the needy, the big bosses keep everything for themselves. And people have to hitch a ride to São Paulo in the back of a truck so they won't starve to death. I kept thinking about all that on the way back. It's truly appalling. Luckily things are different in Minas.

Well, Mom, I'll stop here for now.
Hugs for everyone, and a special one for you.
Your son,

Célio

Diadema, March 10, 1974

Mom,

I was so happy you remembered my birthday. We didn't have a party, but yesterday Nena, Mr. Válter, Mrs. Germana, Eliane and I went out for a pizza. Nena gave me a really nice leather wallet with a bunch of different compartments. Now I need a picture of you and Dad to put in it.

Things are pretty normal around here, Mom. Nena is teaching at a private school in São Bernardo because the pay is better and we want to see if this year we can make a down payment on that plot of land I told you about. I even sold my vacation time with that in mind. I must confess I feel uneasy about things, though, because I'm afraid that Nena will eventually meet someone who's better off than me, who isn't a blue-collar worker like I am, and then she'll leave me. But I know I can't hold her back either. Mrs. Germana says the world is changing and women can't just stay holed up in their houses waiting for their husbands to come home from work. She says if she could, and if she had the education, she'd go out and find a job too. I don't argue anymore, you know how people from Ceará are feisty. But deep down I'm honestly afraid about what the future might bring.

Does Lúcia really have another boyfriend? I'd pay to see that. What she needs to do is come to her senses and help out more around the house. And is Luizinho still following Dad around in the evangelical church? Isn't Dad ashamed to be exposing his family to this kind of embarrassment? I honestly don't understand it.

I'm supposed to meet up with Nilson next week. We're planning to go see a movie with Giuliano Gemma. Do you remember how much I used to like the movies? I was always hanging out at the Edgard Cinema. I loved trading magazines at the door and then catching a matinee. I miss those days, Mom, I really do. Those days when, as the song goes, I was happy then and didn't know it.

This year is the World Cup. Everyone here is already buzzing about it. They don't think we're going to win this year . . . We'll see . . .

Célio

Diadema, June 22, 1974

Mom,

Have you all been following the World Cup matches? What a sorry team, two 0–0 ties with Yugoslavia and Scotland. We'll see how it goes against Zaire today. We've got to score big or else . . .*

Sorry for not writing sooner, Mom, but I've been busier than you can imagine. I've been looking at a plot of land in a neighborhood called Jardim Inamar. Mr. Válter told me he would help me with a good down payment to lower the installments, we'll see. I'm feeling a bit down. Things between Nena and me aren't going so well. We fight a lot, we don't have the same opinions about things, she's getting more and more outspoken. This business of teaching classes is messing with her head, I think, it's because of the people she spends time with. Now she's decided she wants to explore more of São Paulo, so every weekend she wants me to take her out to the movies, walk around downtown, go shopping, those kinds of things. She bought a three-in-one sound system and has been listening to loud music, rock, things like that. Even Mr. Válter pointed out this change to her. She says she wants to be independent, not to depend on a husband. I'm not sure where this is headed. Meanwhile, even just to avoid disappointing Mr. Válter, I'm still looking at plots of land. Mrs. Germana has shown her true colors. She supports everything Nena does. You did warn me that there was something up with her. You were absolutely right.

The other day something strange happened to a guy who lives in the same boarding house as me, Norivaldo. He's a chatty

*Brazil beat Zaire 3–0 and advanced to the next round. By some miracle they managed to finish in fourth place in that World Cup.

little guy, kind of the type who always butts in, you know? Apparently he was walking on a street when the mounted police passed by. He made fun of the officers, then one of them got down and told him to kiss his horse. He said he wasn't kissing anything, so they carted him off to the police station and gave him a serious beating. Things must have gotten ugly because he showed up at the boarding house all beaten up. I didn't see him but that's what they told me. He grabbed his bag and disappeared, and no one's heard from him since. We have to watch what we say around here. I sure do.

Alright, Mom, I'll say goodbye for now, from your beloved son,

Célio

Mom,*

I knew things weren't going to end well for Uncle Zizinho. The last time I saw him, I'm not sure when it was, he was already drinking like crazy. And when it starts getting like that, there's no hope. I'm really sad, more for Aunt Dilma and the kids than for him. He never liked to work, everyone knew that, and he would take advantage of Aunt Dilma, poor thing. That's why her legs are full of varicose veins, from standing up for hours on end at that corner bar. Lord help me, I've never seen a dirtier place. I went to eat at her house once when the bar was still in their living room, remember? I almost threw up when I saw how dirty it was. And how about the stench? I don't know how they could stand to live in such filth. Maybe Aunt Dilma can try to live a happier life from now on, free from that burden.

Mom, I ended up buying the plot of land. It's small, 10 in front and 20 in back, but it's in a great location. I spent the past few weekends clearing the brush and then last week we put up a barbed wire fence. Mr. Válter is excited, he treats me like a son, but things with Nena are still problematic. But I don't want to make you worry, Mom. I talked to some of my friends and they said that's just the way it is, that life as a couple isn't a bed of roses. They say things will get better later on, but I'm not so sure.

Remember that guy I told you about, Norivaldo? He never did end up coming back. He even left some unpaid bills for Mrs. Sinoca, poor woman. Fabinho, who's always well informed, said the problem is the dictatorship because they arrest people and then they disappear. There are people who like to go wild, too. I just keep to myself. I don't get involved with anyone.

*Though not dated, this letter was probably written on August 18, 1974 because the postmark is from August 19, 1974.

Tell Luizinho that money's a bit tight for now, but at Christmas, God willing, I'll send him what he asked for.

Your son,

Célio

Diadema, November 10, 1974

Mom,

I have some really bad news to give to you and Dad: Nena and I broke up. And it's for good. We even told Mr. Válter and Mrs. Germana, it was a shock to them, especially to Mr. Válter because I think Mrs. Germana was actually hoping this would happen. He was very upset, but he understood my point of view and even apologized to me. Things hadn't been going well for some time and Nena and I couldn't even have a decent conversation anymore. All we did was fight. The thing that set it off was when I bought the plot of land. Because from my point of view, that meant a commitment to our future, almost like an engagement. I said that to her, that the next step was for us to get engaged, and the first thing she said was that this whole idea of engagement was old-fashioned and so on. So we argued, because I thought she was just looking for an excuse to break up. Then I kept pushing, and she ended up admitting that she wasn't sure if she really wanted to get married anymore, because she was thinking about going back to school and she wanted to leave Diadema, go live in São Paulo, etc. At that point I got upset and asked her if she thought I was a fool, coming at me with such nonsense after all this time, and waiting until I had bought the plot to tell me all this. So then she started crying, we were in the living room, then Mrs. Germana came in accusing me of hurting her daughter and saying that when something gets off to a bad start it never works out, and so on. Then Mr. Válter showed up and I got mad and said that Nena was ashamed of me because I was a blue-collar worker, and since her father was also a blue-collar worker and so was her brother, she was actually ashamed of all of us. It was complete pandemonium. In the end, she had all the gifts I'd given to her delivered to the boarding house, and she wouldn't even let me in when I went over to drop off the gifts she'd given to me. It was such an awkward situation, I even got drunk for the first time in my life. Anyway, I put up a For Sale sign on the lot and as soon as I can sell it I'll pay Mr. Válter back what I owe him and that will be the end of it.

Please don't worry about me, Mom. I'm fine. It was for the best.

Célio

Diadema, November 24, 1974

Mom,

I was shocked at what you told me about Marina. What she did is a crime. Do you mean to tell me that no one noticed she was pregnant? That's impossible, Mom. Not even in the beginning, when women get morning sickness? And now what? How is she going to raise a child like that who has so many problems? Not to mention doing it on her own and with such a bad reputation? I'm not sure I understood: did she keep a belt tied around her waist? And the belt made the child deformed? And what about Godmother? She must be devastated, poor woman. It's a shame Godfather is a pushover. If it was me, I would go after the guy who did it and kill him. I would go to the ends of the earth to find him. I would finish him off for good.

You don't have to worry about me. Mr. Válter is still as good a friend as ever, and so is Fabinho. I have no desire to hear about Nena. I hope she's happy with the path she's chosen, that's it. The other day I took a little gift over to Eliane and drank a beer with Mr. Válter. He was really upset about what happened. I can't stand Mrs. Germana anymore. What a shrew. But I don't wish anything bad on her. Someday she'll have to answer for filling her daughter's head with nonsense, that's for sure.

Some things are a blessing in disguise, though. God willing, this year I'll spend Christmas and New Year's there with all of you. Go ahead and start getting ready because we're going to have one heck of a celebration.

Célio

Diadema, January 12, 1975

Mom,

I made it back safe and sound. The return trip is always tough because as the years pass by it gets harder and harder for me to think about going back to live there in Cataguases. This time I hung around town a bit more, saw some old friends, ran into others who are also living here in São Paulo and my feeling is that I won't ever go back. It's a really sad thought because I don't belong here. But I also feel like I don't belong over there anymore either. In other words, I don't belong anywhere. That hurts deep down inside. I was coming back on the bus, the night sky full of stars, and I couldn't even sleep. I have so many things on my mind. Mr. Volfe, who's now head of the company but still as nice as ever, saw that I was looking glum and came over to talk to me. He gave me some advice and said that he also feels the same way, living in a place that's so far away from where he was born, where they don't even speak the same language—he has such a weird way of speaking, but I'm used to it now. In the beginning I could hardly understand a thing. It was good to talk to him, but after I broke up with Nena I started feeling lonelier than ever, because while we were dating I stopped hanging out with the guys from the boarding house and even the guys at work. I stopped playing soccer with them and going places with them and so this is how things are now.

People are going to a place nearby called Praia Grande for Carnival and they invited me. Maybe I'll go with them, even though I don't like all the Carnival madness. They said they're going just to relax, though, so I think I'll join them. But don't worry, I know how to take good care of myself.

Célio

Mom, I'm thinking of spending Holy Week at the farm in Rodeiro, what do you think? Would you be able to go?

(I liked Paulinho a lot. I think Lúcia is in good hands. We remembered that we played a lot of pick-up soccer together when we used to live in Vila Teresa. I hope Lúcia gets it right with him and they stay together.)

Diadema, May 11, 1975

Mom,

I'm still struck by what we saw in the countryside. Back in the day we used to walk that stretch to Grandpa's house and every now and then we'd see a house, a dog at the gate, people out in the fields, crops, cattle. Now there's nothing left. It's so quiet you don't even hear a single bird anymore. How long will Uncle Antônio last out there? The boys have all gone off to Ubá, he's the only one working there, and Mauro and Mauricinho haven't left yet because they're not old enough. But as soon as they get the chance they'll leave him there to fend for himself, mark my words. And would that be so wrong? Not at all. There's nothing left to do out there in the countryside, unfortunately. It's a shame because I remember how much fun we used to have in the old days. We had to take turns sleeping at each house so that no one would get jealous. I remember slaughtering pigs, making fresh mango and guava jams, making homemade *doce de leite*, picking corn, threshing beans, harvesting rice, snapping off tobacco stalks, milking the cows . . . We were busy all day and night. And we'd go fishing, play soccer, play hide and seek . . . Now there's nothing left. It's a crying shame. I was shocked by the whole thing. And what about the houses by the roadside? I don't know if you noticed, but they're all falling apart. Those crosses on the doors are useless now. To be honest, I've decided I'm never going to set foot there again. I can't stand to see all that desolation. I came back here sadder than I was when I left.

Speaking of which, I'm going to move to a new place. I went to look at a boarding house in Piraporinha and I think I'll move there. I want to have my own room. This situation of sharing a room, a closet, all those things, it isn't working for me anymore. I'm too old for it. At this Piraporinha boarding house everyone has a key to the front door and another one for their room. It's safer and more convenient, too. Poor Mrs. Sinoca doesn't know this yet. She's going to be disappointed, but I have to think of myself sometimes.

    With your blessing, your son,

                                                    Célio

Diadema, May 25, 1975

Mom,

I'm taking a vacation starting on June 15th. I'm going with one of my friends from work, Gilcimar, to his parents' house in Taiobeiras, a town in the north of Minas. I'll spend 15 days there and then come to Cataguases. So, you can expect me at the end of June, I'll be there. Tell Dad to buy some duck because I'm dying to eat duck. I haven't had any since the days when we ate it out in the countryside, back when Grandpa was still alive. And tell Lúcia I was really happy to hear that she's thinking about getting engaged. Paulinho is a serious, honest and hardworking guy, and that's what matters.

Besides that, everything's fine.

Don't tell Luizinho but I'm bringing him an official Palmeiras shirt and a pair of official cleats, too. I bet no one in Cataguases has anything like it. He's going to love them.

Your son asks for your blessing,

Célio

Diadema, August 10, 1975

Mom,

I agree, it was the best vacation of my life too. I was really happy to see that you're doing so well, and to see how nice the house looks now with the walls painted blue. I've got to hand it to you, Mom, you have good taste. Now that you have the electric pump no one has to pull water up from the well anymore. Who would have thought that Dad, out there selling pastry cones, would be able to buy a pump, right? I could tell you liked the refrigerator. I had been wanting to buy you one for a long time, but I never managed to save up enough money before. Now you can have cold water from the fridge whenever you want, all you have to do is open the door. I thought it was really funny that people were showing up to get ice. Then I remembered we used to do that a lot too, didn't we? Life sure can take some interesting turns . . .

I've been thinking a lot about what you said and you're absolutely right. Now that I have my own room, I'm going to try to be more organized. I was looking pretty sloppy, I'm glad you pointed it out. But I promise to pay more attention to my appearance. Just so you know, yesterday I went to see a movie in São Paulo, and on the way I decided to have my picture taken. That's when I saw I needed a haircut . . . Well, to make a long story short, what was supposed to be a trip to the movies turned into something else. I even bought a new shirt, so I can look nice when I go out here in Diadema. For the time being, though, I honestly think I'm done with dating for a while.

With your blessing, Mom, your beloved son,

Célio

Diadema, November 2, 1975

Mom,

Tomorrow it will have been a year since Nena and I broke up. And today is All Souls' Day. It's raining a lot here. It's like this every All Souls' Day, isn't it? It always rains like crazy. And I have to admit that I'm sad. Yes, I've been receiving your letters, and I hope you can forgive me, but I just don't feel like doing anything lately. I go to the company, work, come back to my room, study. Right now I'm reading a four-volume Mechanical Technology Manual that Mr. Volfe told me to read. But when the weekend comes around and everyone's planning all sorts of things, fishing at Billings, lunch at someone or other's house, a trip down to Praia Grande, a stroll around São Paulo, I never get excited about any of it. Most of the time these things end with everyone getting drunk, playing the guitar and crying their eyes out. It's just so incredibly sad. In moments like these I understand Fabinho's anger. He always says that he doesn't understand why we have to move so far away from the people we love in order to make a living. I completely agree with him, I think the world is really unfair. Over there in Cataguases when the kids from rich families go away to study they know that sooner or later they'll come back as doctors, engineers, executives or lawyers. But those of us who are poor leave and never return. That's why they say rich people smile for no reason. That's exactly why, because they're always close to their families, that's why.

Mom, I'm sorry if this letter makes you worry. I'm only going to mail it because I know it's been a while since you've heard from me. But please don't worry, apart from all that I'm fine.

Your son,

Célio

Diadema, November 15, 1975

Mom,

I have some good news. I went to visit Mrs. Glenda at the boarding house on Sunday and Nilson was there. We had a great time. He's doing really well, making good money, he even bought a car, a VW Bug. We decided that we're going to travel together to Cataguases for New Year's. So go ahead and start making that *taioba* I like so much, and the cookie pie, and the stuffed chicken. Tell Dad to buy a case of beer and a liter bottle of that Pedra Lisa *cachaça* because I'll be there soon.

Nilson told me he and Toninha are still together and they definitely plan to get married. But from the way he talks about it, I'm actually not so sure. He's still that same mischievous kid he's always been. He did say he bought a plot of land in Ibraim, though, and next year they'll start pouring the foundation for the house. But what I didn't understand is that he wouldn't be moving back to Cataguases anytime soon. That means he's either going to bring Toninha to live here or he's going to make her wait until he retires. And that will take a while.

Mrs. Glenda is doing well, she sends her love. I need to go see Mrs. Sinoca one of these days, I heard she's having some problems with diabetes, but I just don't have the time or energy.

A hug from your son,

Célio

Diadema, January 11, 1976

Mom,

Thank God we made it here safe and sound, the car didn't break down on the way back. Nilson was mad because he had to spend a fortune to fix the Bug's engine. He said he's going to go after the guy who sold him the car because he took advantage of him. He got a lemon, poor Nilson.

Mom, it's too bad things didn't work out the way we wanted them to. The fact that Dad is having trouble breathing is serious. Do you think it's his heart? Has he gone back to see the doctor? The tuberculosis might have come back as well, because he's coughing up blood like he did when he had tuberculosis. Just when we think we're out of the woods, somehow we're right back in again. God forgive me for saying this, but I'm beginning to question whether or not God really exists. Because sometimes I think that if he does, he only protects the rich. The poor are left to fend for themselves. I'm not going to say anything else because I know you don't like to hear it, you think it's blasphemous, but on the inside, I won't lie to you, I feel more and more outraged.

At least there's the good news about Lúcia's wedding. I'm going to save up to pay for her ceremony and reception. I want the whole church to be all decorated and I even talked to Father Rodolfo, from the São José Operário Church, we've arranged to have his youth group sing at the ceremony. The reception will be at the Senai Alumni Club, leave the arrangements to me because I know the people there, they're all friends of mine from when I was at Senai. I'll take care of everything. It's going to be a high-class affair, you'll see.

I also enjoyed seeing Luzimar. He's really grown into quite a handsome young man. I did what you asked and talked to him about his chances of getting a position here in São Paulo. I also told him that, if he wants, I could try to find something for him here in Diadema, although it will be harder since he doesn't have any training. If he at least liked to study, then it would be easier, but he thought he could make a living anyway, so what can we do, right? All this to say I got him to open his eyes a bit. He's turning 18 this year and it's time to start thinking about the future.

Luizinho is a great kid, Mom. I was amazed at how much he knows. He says that now that he's passed at Senai his dream is to finish up the course so he can get a job. I'm not worried about him at all because his head is in the right place and he's going to do just fine in his career.

I paid cash for the TV set with my salary bonus, Mom, don't worry. Now you can relax and watch your *telenovela*, you need it. My hope is that you'll be able to stop washing clothes for hire, but I know you don't want to give up on having some of your own spending money, without having to rely on Dad. I think you could at least consider dropping some of the orders to lighten your load, just a thought. Think about it.

Mom, please let me know how things are going with Dad.

A hug from your son,

Célio

Diadema, March 7, 1976

Mom,

I think it's outrageous that Dad only managed to get an appointment with Doctor Pace for February! Just because he's poor, it's okay to make him wait, is that it? That's why so many people die without getting the help they need. It's as if the government thinks poor people are just trash, like they're nothing. When do the test results come in? As soon as they do, please write to me right away because I want to know. Tell Lúcia to stop all this talk of postponing the wedding. That won't do anyone any good. I've already planned my vacation time for May and I ordered the invitations from a fancy printing shop here in São Bernardo, with red envelopes and embossed lettering, it's really something. I hope she likes it. They'll be ready in a week and I've already found someone to deliver them to you. I've arranged everything at the Senai Alumni Club, the hall is reserved for the 22nd of May and everything will work out just fine, God willing. I need to set the price with the youth group, but Luizinho knows them so he can take care of that himself.

Fabinho came to see me the other day, he's involved with the union now and he wants me to participate in the meetings. I told him I'm just going to wait until all this wedding chaos is over and we know more about what's wrong with Dad, because right now my head's not in the right place for this. But it's not rioting or anything, don't worry. It's all completely legal and the people are connected to the Church.

During our conversation I ended up asking about Mr. Válter, who's been on leave for a long time now. Apparently he has high blood pressure and something going on with his heart. He said he's taking it in stride and misses me a lot, that kind of thing. I asked about Eliane, who's a young woman now, according to him, and about Mrs. Germana who hasn't changed, and also about Nena, who's engaged to a guy who works at the VW office. It seems she was through with blue-collar workers. I promised to visit someday soon, because I really like Mr. Válter, I owe a lot to him.

That's it, Mom, I'll stop here, goodbye for now, your son,

Célio

Diadema, March 14, 1976

Mom,

Here we go again, trying to grab a bull by the horns. Some life we're living, isn't it? This whole thing of Dad needing surgery to remove a lung is just awful. But if he needs the operation, it's better to do it soon. We can't put it off. Let me know when you set the date, so I can run over to Juiz de Fora to be there for it. You must be spending a lot on these trips there, right? If you need money, borrow some from Mr. Zé Pinto and I'll pay him back. I've talked to the people here at work and I'm going to sell 15 vacation days to help with things over there. Did Lúcia receive the invitations? Did she like them?

Mrs. Sinoca died on Friday. Yesterday I went to the funeral. I was sad that I didn't go to see her in the hospital. I liked her a lot, she was such an important person to me here. But I was glad to see that there were so many people at the funeral. I met up with some of my friends from the boarding house and Gilcimar was there too, I don't know if you remember him, I went on vacation with him to a town in the north of Minas, I can't remember the name. Gilcimar is working at Mercedes now. He got married, has a little son, and is living in São Bernardo. I'm supposed to go visit him one of these days.

Goodbye for now, I miss you, your son,

Célio

(With all this rushing around I almost forgot my birthday. Thanks for remembering, Mom. I loved the little present.)

Diadema, April 25, 1976

Mom,

In times like these we have to be strong and keep it together. What Doctor Pace meant was that Dad definitely has at least six months to live. He's obviously not God to say whether he'll last 1 more year or 50. And I personally think that behind Dad's frail body there's a strength greater than anyone realizes. A person who has beaten hunger, paratyphoid fever, tuberculosis, humiliation, all of these struggles, can make it through this, too. If he can't gain weight anymore, no problem, he doesn't have to. Now Social Security has no excuse not to give him his retirement benefits, unless the medical board thinks that living with one lung is normal. But they won't have the nerve to do that, especially since the decision will come straight from Juiz de Fora, where people take things more seriously.

I told Lúcia the wedding has to happen no matter what, because what if Dad suddenly dies, then at least he can see his daughter get married and die a happy man. So, now that the worst is over, let's focus on the wedding. What still needs to be taken care of? I'll be arriving on the 15th in the morning. I'll have a week to tie up any loose ends. I want you to make manicure, pedicure and hair appointments for yourself and for Lúcia, and not with those girls right there in Paraíso. Choose a beauty salon on the main street, one of those fancy ones where the rich people in Cataguases go. Mom, please, I insist, I really do. And tell Luizinho to be prepared because I'm going to take him with me to the barber on Rui Barbosa Square for a haircut and a facial. For both of us. We're going to clean up all that acne on his face and find a whole bunch of girlfriends for him, you'll see. He won't want to go, I know how he is, but just tell him to stop being silly.

Mom, I'm sending some money with this letter, for what we talked about in Juiz de Fora.

Goodbye for now, your son,

Célio

Diadema, June 20, 1976

Mom,

Tell Lúcia she doesn't have to thank me. I was happy to do it, because family is family, and we only have one in this life. It sure was a great party. It's a shame Dad couldn't be there. Thank God he's already back at home recovering, and pretty soon he'll be his old feisty self again, doing all the things he likes to do. The pain in his ribs is normal. I talked to Doctor Pace and he said that in order to take the lung out they have to lift up the ribcage, and that makes it hurt like crazy afterwards. All he has to do is be careful and do everything that Doctor Pace said, and he'll be as good as new in no time.

I was really happy to see the whole family again. Paulinho looked like a real gent in that suit, didn't he? He came over to thank me, but I told him that you were the one who had offered it as a gift. He believed me, I think. The only bad thing was Luizinho getting drunk, but everyone thought it was funny, so I let it go, he's just a kid trying to act grown up. But he learned his lesson. I'm sure he won't go near fig-leaf liqueur ever again.

I told Lúcia that since she's unemployed, we could buy her a second-hand sewing machine if she wants one. Didn't she take a sewing course with Mrs. Marta? She didn't give me an answer, though. Maybe you could follow up with her and let me know what she says.

Mom, I'll say goodbye for now, from your beloved son,

Célio

Diadema, October 17, 1976

Mom,

You are absolutely right, I haven't been paying enough attention to the family, but you wouldn't believe how busy I've been, Mom. I hardly have time for anything. And it's not because of a girlfriend, like you were thinking. I haven't even had time for that.

I was really happy to hear that Dad's making progress. I told you, Mom, once everyone else has given up, that's when he'll find his own strength to go on. It's amazing. Sometimes I think his religious ways help a lot, too. They're a bit fanatic, but maybe that can be a good thing somehow.

I saw Mr. Válter a while back. You wouldn't believe how far gone he is, Mom. His health has gotten worse, they had to put a pacemaker in his heart, he's so thin and pale, you can hardly imagine. I felt so sorry for him. Having seen him strong and full of energy, and then seeing the way he is now, it just breaks your heart. We talked a little. He complained that I never came back to visit them, but deep down he knows I don't want to go stirring up the past. Life goes on, after all. But he was happy to hear that I'm still friends with Fabinho. In fact, Fabinho got in touch with me again about the union thing. He said the management at Conforja respects me and that my coworkers also like me a lot, so I'm seen as a leader and that could really help the salary campaign for next year. We'll see. Besides that, Fabinho asked me if I might be interested in teaching some classes for people who want to learn about mechanics. I told him I wasn't a teacher, but he said everyone knows that I study a lot and I'd be teaching a subject I know, which is mechanical drawing. Just to see if I'd be any good at it, I taught a class the other day in the lecture hall, a class about how to read a caliper. Everyone really seemed to like it, so I'm going to teach mechanical drawing classes at night to a group of people there. It's a mix of really young guys and even some older men with gray hair, would you believe that?

Alright, Mom, hugs for everyone, I miss you, from your son,

Célio

Diadema, December 5, 1976

Mom,

I'll be able to spend New Year's there with you after all. It wasn't looking good for a while because money is a bit tight, but you can count on me, I'll be there. I won't be bringing any presents this time, but I insist that we have turkey for Christmas dinner. Check where you can get it, then buy it and I'll pay you back. I'll be moving to another boarding house at the beginning of the year. There's a guy who moved here, and the union people told me he can't be trusted because he's an informant for the Federal Police. They say he's living in Diadema to spy on us and turn us in to the government, because you know we're living under a dictatorship that arrests and kills workers who only want to change the unfair situation in this country. But don't say anything about it in Cataguases, otherwise they might arrest you and call you a communist.

Mom, I think you should tear up these letters, in case someone finds them and reads them and tries to cause trouble.

I should be there on the morning of the 22nd, God willing.

Your son,

                                                                      Célio

Diadema, March 13, 1977

Mom,

I did write a letter as soon as I got back here from the Christmas holidays. It must have gotten lost, or worse, it might have been confiscated, because now they open personal mail and go after workers. I'm glad there wasn't anything compromising in the letter.

I'm happy to hear that Dad is already thinking about starting to sell his snacks again. But tell him they have to be light: doughnuts, cookies, pastry cones, cassava puffs, crusty rolls, that kind of thing.

Mom, listen to this! Nena is getting married. Fabinho told me the week before last and I asked if she was going to send me an invitation. He dodged my question, but I already have it all planned out: even if she does invite me I won't go. But I'm going to buy her a nice present. A blender or an electric mixer, something she'll have to use all the time and every time she does she'll remember that I was the one who gave it to her. Despite everything, I do like her. She's a good person, she's just stuck up and thinks she's better than everyone else. She's going to have a lot of trouble in life.

This boarding house isn't as good as the other one. It's more like a small hotel, but it'll do for now. I don't like moving around from place to place like this. When I find something better then I'll move.

On the 4th we had a meeting to discuss the list of demands for this year's salary campaign. It was really cool, there were tons of people there. And now we're planning a big party for May Day on the 1st. I think this year it's going to catch on.

Mom, I'm going to take time off in July this year, to coincide with Luizinho's vacation. I was thinking that maybe we could all go to Marataízes this year, including Dad. Wouldn't that be great?

Think about it and let me know.

Your son,

Célio

Diadema, May 29, 1977

Mom,

It's true, Nena's wedding is in July, that's why I don't want to be here then. I wanted to go to Marataízes, but I understand that Dad can't travel and you don't want to leave him alone, but Luizinho could go with me. What's he going to do out in the countryside? There's nothing left there. But if he doesn't want to go with me, that's fine. I'll think about what to do instead. I think I might end up going by myself anyway.

The May Day celebration was unforgettable. We're really excited about the salary campaign. We'll see how it turns out.

I'm going to leave this boarding house after all. Fabinho referred me to a woman named Neilane in the Serraria neighborhood, who rents a room in her house. It's not a boarding house, she's a widow with two children and she rents out the room to help pay the bills. She serves breakfast and dinner, and the room is really nice, very clean and tidy. I might move in as early as next week.

Célio

Diadema, August 14, 1977

Mom,

They say God works in mysterious ways and it must be true. If I hadn't given up on the idea of going to Marataízes and spent my vacation there at home I never would have met Celeste. You saw what a cool girl she is, right, Mom? And how about that moped of hers? Isn't it great? She really liked you, and I was happy because it seemed like you liked her too, right? Too bad we only met during my last week there. But I gave her my address and she said she'd write to me, so we'll see. She told me she already knew Dad pretty well because her mother used to buy pastry cones from him. But, to be fair, who doesn't know Dad in Cataguases, right?

I enjoyed seeing Lúcia. She seems to be doing well. That place where she's living is a bit odd. I think I'd be afraid of living below a spiritualist center. And don't you think it's really close to the river? But she seemed happy and that's what matters. I hardly spoke to Luizinho. He came in from the countryside and got together with his friends from the youth group. Mom, those guys don't smoke pot, do they? Some of them just have that look! Especially the one who plays guitar, what's his name again?

Mom, if this thing with Celeste works out, maybe I'll get excited and buy a plot there in Paraíso and start building a little house in a few years. It would be a dream come true!

Goodbye for now, I miss you,

Célio

Diadema, October 9, 1977

Mom,

September was a difficult month for us. No one let on, but we managed to rally a huge crowd in our campaign for the restitution of the 34.1%, that is, to restore the part of our salary that the government stole from us as workers. The union people were thrilled because the older workers said they hadn't seen anything like this happen since the dictatorship began. Now we're going to start making plans for next year. Everyone's excited and people are saying that things are really going to take off now.

Celeste hasn't written to me at all, Mom. I guess it was just a flash in the pan. I'd bet she was already making fun of me the moment I left. As pretty as she is, she probably wants to marry a rich guy from the city. But, it's alright, we're going to show who's really running this country now. Just let it be.

Everything's going well here. I've settled right in at Mrs. Neilane's house. Her kids are really nice. They're steelworkers too. Analice works at Villares and Joãozinho works at VW. The food isn't all that great, but you can't have everything you want in life, right?

Hugs for you and Dad, and give my love to Lúcia, Paulinho and Luizinho.

Your son,

Célio

Diadema, November 15, 1977

Mom,

November is proving to be a sad month. On the 4th I received your letter saying that Aunt Dilma died. That made me
really sad. I even sent a telegram to the kids, did they mention it?
And then on the 10th Mr. Válter passed away. I went to the wake
and saw Mrs. Germana there, she's a wreck. Time flies by and we
don't even notice it, you know? Just the other day she was full of
life, stubborn as they come, and now it's like she's aged over-
night. You wouldn't even recognize her now, she looks so different. Fabinho is devastated, poor guy. I didn't see Eliane, not even
at the funeral. I also ran into Nena and her husband. We said
hello but it was kind of awkward. I didn't really talk to her, just
gave my condolences and snuck out.

No, Mom, Celeste really hasn't written to me. Forget about
her. She's out of the picture.

I don't know the two priests who were kicked out of town,
no. But they must have been up to no good, don't you think? I
think they taught at Cataguases High School, but I never met
them. Maybe if I saw them I'd recognize their faces, but just
hearing their names, I'm not sure.

Mom, I'll say goodbye for now, your son,

Célio

(I'm probably going to stay here for the holidays. Mrs. Neilane invited me for Christmas dinner and the union folks are
celebrating New Year's Eve at Praia Grande. I think I'll go with
them.)

Diadema, February 5, 1978

Mom,

I have big news: I bought a car! Fabinho introduced me to a guy who was desperate to sell a '72 VW Bug with a 1500-cylinder engine, so I put a down payment on it and now I just owe a bit more that I'll take out of my vacation pay. I've already driven it a bunch of times and pretty soon I'll be racing around like a rocket. The car is Saturn yellow and it's in really good condition. It's a gem, you've got to see it.

Things here are heating up. Our demonstration on the 1st of May is going to be a real show of force. I've planned to take my vacation from March 15th to April 15th because I want to make sure I'm here to see the inauguration of the union's new president on the 21st and to participate in the preparations for our May Day party.

I miss you, your son,

Célio

Diadema, March 5, 1978*

Mom,

I've made plans with one of my colleagues who lives in Mutum and we're going to try the car out on the highway. I got my license last week and I'm driving like a pro. We'll take turns behind the wheel until we get to Leopoldina. I'll drop him off there and he'll take a bus to Mutum. Everything's all lined up, don't worry. I'm going to drive halfway, then I'll sleep while he drives to Leopoldina so that I'll be rested to drive the rest of the way to Cataguases. And since we're not in any hurry to get there, if we get tired we'll just pull over to the side of the road and get some sleep, don't worry. I can't wait for all of you to see the car. You know how I like fine details, so I added some extras here and there, like hubcaps, and I put on chenille seat covers, had the engine cleaned with castor oil, polished it, it's just beautiful. I never imagined I would like a car this much.

Alright, Mom, sending you all my love, I miss you, from your beloved son,

Célio

*This was the last letter written by my brother. His friend—if he existed—did not go with him. I say "if he existed" because sometimes I find myself wondering whether it hadn't been his intention all along to go alone, and perhaps he made up the driving companion just so my mother wouldn't worry. The highway police told us that he probably fell asleep at the wheel, crossed over to the other side of the road and was crushed under an oncoming truck. What matters is that he left us a week after his twenty-sixth birthday, opening a wound that would never heal.

Appendix

03/15/2008

Célio:

I was awakened at 7am this morning by a phone call from Lúcia reminding me that today marks the 30th anniversary of your death. She was emotional and she cried, perhaps mixing genuine longing for someone she loved and sorrow for the hardships life has thrown at her over all these years, which, believe me, have been neither few nor easy. I hung up, sat down on the living room sofa and, a decade after having quit smoking, I felt an overwhelming urge to smoke again, which I managed to resist with extreme difficulty.

I regret that we had so little time together. I was ten years old when you left for Diadema, along with hundreds of other recent graduates from Senai. A mass of pimple-faced teenagers who had never gone beyond the hills that surround Cataguases, packing into the buses chartered by companies in São Paulo, abandoning heartbroken mothers and girlfriends who hoped for the success of your venture while contradictorily aching for your return, a return that would never come to pass. To come back would mean to fail, and for those young men who had nothing, there was absolutely no way they would let anything derail their dreams. In the beginning they would still visit their families quite regularly, but little by little, their ties to the small town with no prospects began to fray: many would take with them siblings, parents, friends, while others would form new bonds of friendship or romance, chipping away at the frequency of their visits to Cataguases for long weekends or the Christmas holidays. Back then we were divided into "the ones who had already left" and "the ones who weren't old enough to do it yet"...

I belonged to the second group and proudly prepared myself to follow in your footsteps. I would go to school, play pick-up soccer, run errands, and every time I went down to the main street I would always stop at the Bar do Auzílio to check if there was a letter from you, which I would excitedly read to Mom with relish, tripping over words and stammering through the embarrassing parts. One of them caused a real uproar at home—the one when you announced that you were bringing your girlfriend Nena with you on vacation to meet the family, along with her sister Eliane and their mother, whose name escapes me now. Those days in March of 1973 were perhaps the most hectic of our lives. Mom was busy running back and forth, giving chaotic orders: "Luizinho, go to Beira-Rio and buy this," "Luizinho, go to the main street and buy that," stocking up on things like olives, canned peas, salami, mayonnaise, apples, all of those luxuries you were used to in São Paulo and that had never found their way into our pantry.

She would anxiously agonize: "Do you think Nena's mother likes cookie pie?," "And what about Nena? Do you think she's a picky girl?," "Do you think the younger sister eats vegetables?" In the end, everything fell into place. She and Nena's mother would spend the day in front of the stove, each trying to outdo the other's cooking skills in a veiled competition. Nervous and still recovering from the tuberculosis that would cost him a lung a few years later, Dad kept his distance, as if invisible. And Lúcia, we were all worried about rebellious, temperamental, feisty Lúcia, "Do you think she'll act up?," we wondered, but in the end she was on her best behavior, acting friendly toward Nena and maternal with Eliane. Ah, Eliane, my first love . . . ! I was foolishly infatuated, ready to fulfill her every wish . . . Like a saint, not a single rude word ever came out of my mouth, carefully seeking to live up to the image of the ideal son that everyone saw in you . . . When you left I spent days sulking around in corners. I would go up to the field in Paraíso, the Pomba River down below, the blue hills in the distance, eager for the time to pass more swiftly so my turn would come to break away too, go to São

Paulo, get rich, and never show my face in that dream-crushing place again ... April, however, brought other interests and my life quickly got back on track ...

The last time we got together was in August of 1977. We didn't know that we would never see you again, not even lying in a coffin, to Mom's heartache, we weren't allowed to open it due to the condition of your body after that senseless accident, almost a year later, in which you veered your VW Bug under a truck that was coming from Recife. That August became crystallized in a photograph, the only one in which we appear together, a slightly out-of-focus portrait that was taken by someone or other at Rui Barbosa Square, and that now adorns the bookshelf in my living room. You are standing arm in arm with Celeste whom you had recently met, both smiling, I'm in front of the two of you, and behind us is a *sibipiruna* tree and half of a popcicle cart.

We never heard from Nena again, or her mother, or Eliane ... It's funny how for me, it feels like they never really existed in time, but only in that specific moment, as if created to provide a rare instance of happiness in our tragedy-ridden family. I don't remember faces, clothing, situations, nothing, just the echoing voices suspended in a universe without clocks or ages. In the photograph of us together, however, time is present: your eyes are focused on the photographer, and what we see is the image of someone who seemed to know that he would never reach his full potential. Celeste got married, moved to Vitória, had two children, grew old ... I've grown older, too, we all have ... All except you, who will forever be 26 years old, burning inexorably in my memories.

Luiz Ruffato

Translator's Note

I have been a reader and admirer of Luiz Ruffato's fiction for two decades. I first read his work in transit, as I commuted by bus and subway between Providence, Rhode Island, and Cambridge, Massachusetts, three days a week. At the time I was teaching Portuguese language and culture classes at Harvard University. It was during this period that I began an e-mail correspondence with Ruffato, and promptly learned of his generous capacity for dialogue. To translate Ruffato's fiction is to rely soundly on the author's unselfish, creative spirit.

Luiz Ruffato's storytelling is a political act. Reliant on formal experimentation, he aims to capture the vast scope of Brazil's human registers on the page. His writing expresses landscapes, thoughts, dialogues, emotions, materiality, memories, aspirations, injustices, regrets: belonging and un-belonging on equal footing, each given voice almost in a single breath. Ruffato's innovations in form include changes in typography designed to signal shifts in timeframes; passages interrupted by dialogues or inner thoughts; scenery and interior settings described in inven-

tive list forms; and sentences that end abruptly, or with varia-
tions in punctuation.

As an avid reader of world literature, Ruffato shares
twentieth-century American writer William Faulkner's attention to cadence and diction, as well as a narrative style character-
ized by a complex and pluriphonic stream of consciousness. In
Unremembering Me we see examples of this style in his elegiac
prologue, "A Necessary Explanation." The letters that follow
share a formal structure with the work of eighteenth-century
French writer Pierre Choderlos de Laclos. In Laclos' epistolary
novel *Les Liaisons dangereuses*, letters paint an intimate portrait
of individuals caught in a tale of intrigue of sociopolitical and
moral proportions. Ruffato alters the formal epistolary arrange-
ment by composing letters deprived of a response. This formal
framework replicates the acute absence that hovers around the
text.

In each of Luiz Ruffato's works of fiction, there is a strong
emphasis on regional orality and verbal tonality. As someone
who grew up in Brazil's southeast state of Minas Gerais, I was
particularly captivated by Ruffato's *mineiro* timbre. To translate
his fiction is a challenge, even this epistolary novel, despite its
colloquial style. In response to my persistent questions, Luiz
Ruffato extended his unwavering support, such as how to translate Minas regionalisms like "muxiada" (melancholic) or "cara-
mujos" (a type of dry, crusty roll), or how to select the exact yellow of Célio's 1972 VW Beetle. Through it all, I endeavored to
express Célio's voice and personality in English: his strong sense
of responsibility coupled with unworldly immaturity; his frus-
trating biases and endearing compassion; his insecure arrogance
and firm sense of duty; his intense longing for home and his
levelheadedness as a blue-collar working man; his traditional
values and his emergence as a union member. As it happens, one
of Célio's last letters signals the historic rise of Luiz Inácio Lula

da Silva—known as Lula—as president of the Steelworkers Union. He went on to become president of Brazil in the early part of the twenty-first century.

In Célio, Ruffato presents a multi-dimensional human being, complete with strengths and shortcomings. This is a coming of age story as well as a story of premature loss. In addition to Célio's letter-writing in the first person, Luiz Ruffato himself inhabits the storyline front and center, wearing his heart and humanity on his sleeve. This is his most personal work of fiction to date.

I firmly believe that it often takes a village to complete a literary translation, such is the collaborative nature of the process. With this conviction in mind, I wish to extend my heartfelt thanks to the entire editing team at Tagus Press, especially to two exceptional individuals: Mario Pereira and Dário Borim. At Smith College, I would like to acknowledge the ongoing inspiration and support of my colleague Malcolm McNee. On the home front, Pamela Petro has been an enthusiastic reader with a keen writer's eye.

In the summer of 2016 I was invited to participate in a Smith write-on-site group led by Velma García and Leslie King. That collective space and sanctuary offered me the rhythm and routine necessary to complete the first draft of this translation, at a time when I was grieving for the loss of my dear mother. Only after the fact did I fully grasp the symmetry of this outcome: between my translation as lamentation and Luiz Ruffato's autobiographical fiction, so heavily conditioned by family loss and bereavement.

This translation is dedicated to my parents *in memoriam*, and to Pamela, in life.

Luiz Ruffato was born in Cataguases, Minas Gerais to an immigrant, working-class family, and today is among the most influential Brazilian writers of his generation. Son of a popcorn vendor and a washerwoman, Ruffato has dedicated his writing to exploring the voices, aspirations, and struggles of his country's urban, working-class communities with tremendous stylistic inventiveness. His 2001 award-winning novel, *Eles eram muitos cavalos* (*There Were Many Horses*), has been translated into English, Finnish, French, German, Italian, Macedonian and Spanish. *De mim já nem se lembra* (*Unremembering Me*) was first published in Brazil in 2007 as part of an education campaign aimed at young adults. It was subsequently published in Portugal (2012) and in translation in Italy (2012) and in Mexico (2018), and is forthcoming in Argentina. It was reissued in Brazil in 2016 as a trade book by Companhia das Letras, in a revised and expanded edition. Luiz Ruffato was the keynote speaker at the 2013 Frankfurt Book Fair, and the 2016 recipient of the Hermann Hesse International Prize in Literature.

Marguerite Itamar Harrison grew up in Minas Gerais, Brazil, the bilingual daughter of a Brazilian mother and an American father. She is an Associate Professor of Portuguese & Brazilian Studies at Smith College, where she has been the recipient of the Sherrerd Distinguished Teaching award. Harrison has been a reader, critic and translator of Luiz Ruffato's work for twenty years. She has published scholarly essays on Ruffato's fiction in *Luso-Brazilian Review* and *Romance Notes*, and translations in *Brasil/Brazil* and *Metamorphoses*. In 2007 she edited the international critical study *Uma Cidade em Camadas* (Horizonte) on Ruffato's acclaimed novel *Eles eram muitos cavalos*.